AM
BANDITS

The Colt's went off.

The slug struck the shouting man high in his chest, broke his shout off in a grunt, and a bone there in a quick crack as the lead went through.

The bandit leader glared at Lee as if he could, by staring dreadfully enough, kill him. He stumbled to a stop no more than ten feet away and carefully lifted his revolver—an old Smith and Wesson Russian .44, Lee saw—to put this bullet where he wished it. And looked steady enough to get it done.

Lee scrambled to his feet like a kicked dog. He took a great stomping leap to the left, spun on his heel, and dove to the right, reaching down into his right boot-top as he did. He rolled, and came to his feet just as the Smith and Wesson went off with a considerable bang. Lee felt a sting at the inside of his left knee—could still stand—palmed the broad-blade dagger in his right hand, drew that hand back like a baseball pitcher, and threw the knife spinning.

The bandit saw it coming. Lee saw the flicker of his eyes, but the man was too badly hurt to go tumbling over the countryside as Lee had for the dodge. He stood stock still (dying, no doubt, from that shot to his chest) and fired the Smith and Wesson as the dagger whacked into his belly—nine inches of broad, double-edge steel—and left him doubled over on his knees, his big revolver fallen into the sand beside him, of no use at all . . . .

Also in the BUCKSKIN Series:

BUCKSKIN #11

TRIGGER GUARD

Roy LeBeau

LEISURE BOOKS ∞ NEW YORK CITY

A LEISURE BOOK

Published by

Dorchester Publishing Co., Inc.
6 East 39th Street
New York, NY 10016

Printed in the United States of America

TRIGGER GUARD

Chapter 1

Juan Soto, as a child in the mountain *pueblo* of San Hermin, had dreamed of being a bandit.

It had seemed to him of all lives the most perfect, the most romantic, the most comfortable. To be always on horseback, to be always fed (and well fed), to have a fine pistol, to have all the prettiest girls staring after him in admiration . . .

So much for the dreams of youth.

The dreams had not encompassed the *Rurales* and their ready nooses or the brutality of his companions, the filth, the desperate need for warmth in bitter mountain winters. The scratching, scrabbling, the murdering for a pitcher of stolen goat's milk, a few *tortillas* wrapped in some peasant's shirt-tail.

A foul business, and too seldon rewarded by the likes of a prize such as this, this treasure on horseback which now rode down the *arroyo* toward them.

The *gringo* rode a small and undistinguished paint, an *Indio* horse, it appeared. But the *norte-americano* was dressed in fine wool and leather, and wore such boots—Juan had seen them clearly when the Yankee stopped for a cup of *mescal* at Las Rosas. Fine tall leather boots. And a superb pistol—a Colt's, of the type called "Bisley."

All this was too much wealth for any one man to possess, wealth sufficient to earn him a cut throat. It was unChristian wealth!

More than sufficient, even without the saddle-bags, those fine tooled-leather bags in which two much smaller leather bags were stuffed. A thousand silver pesos. Perhaps a *thousand* . . .

For this, it was true, they had only the word of Severio's sister, whose husband labored at Don Luis' mine. And this information appeared correct, for since when did the Don's Yankee ride the mountains to no purpose? Never.

And the purpose now? *Banco National* at Paso Robles.

But he would never reach it—nor should he, being not only a *gringo* dog, but an accursed Protestant as well. Let him die here, then, well served for being what he was . . .

It would have been more pleasant to have a larger number of men—these affairs were sometimes surprising—but these three would have to do. Severio, who had the crack-stocked Spenser rifle and kept it to himself as if it were a child (not even allowing Juan to test it with a shot or two); Manuel No-name, a brute from the coast, an Indio who barely understood Spanish; and Mercurio Fuentes, a slender, evil man with unnatural tastes.

These three and no more. A poor following for a man who had, only two years before, robbed the Sinaloa Express train with a band of fifteeen men. True, that deed had not ended well, but at least it had been a deed of significance.

This now, compared to that, was nothing.

It was also a day like a furnace. In this gullied *barranca*, the sun came hammering down hard enough to beat a man into the earth, turning all of Jesus's blessed natural colors on the earth to the harsh tints of hell. The air quivered with the heat, but sent sound only slowly.

Juan could barely hear the hoofbeats of the *gringo's* horse. That doomed one was well in sight now, riding his ugly little *pinto* as if he and all *norte-americanos* owned the very dirt they rode upon.

Coming at a walk, ignorant as a child toddling into a next of *tarantula.*

A fair-enough looking man, it must be admitted. And close enough, too. If the Yankee only turned a little in his saddle, looked up over his right shoulder, then perhaps he would see Juan Soto in the rocks, ready to whistle death down upon him. Young—or almost young, his face clean-shaven as a boy's. He had taken his jacket off—a fine buckskin jacket it was—and rolled it at his saddle cantle with his blanket. A rifle, too. That treasure had been forgotten for a moment; now it was remembered. A shining Winchester rifle. A *General's* weapon. An *Haciendado's* weapon.

And soon to be Juan Soto's weapon. Let Severio brandish his old piece of trash, then!

This *gringo* walking his *pinto* past—and far enough.

Vaya con Dios!

Lee heard the shrill whistle, swung low to the left side of his saddle, and spurred the paint as hard as he could kick. A rifle bullet went droning past, just over his doubled back as the paint, snorting in surprise, bolted to the left, already into a gallop. Down the damn *barranca* he should never have ridden into.

Been riding, day-dreaming like a kid.

Thinking of Rosalia . . . Asking for trouble. And now some other fools had surprised *this* fool.

The little pain was flying, hooves rattling on the stones, the gully's sun-packed sand and dirt. Galloping in a haze of heat and light and dust. The paint canted to the right, leaning as it ran, and Lee swung down further off the saddle, left hand hooked about the horn, ducked lower still, under the racing horse's neck, drew the Bisley from that position, and fired a shot into a huge Mexican lumbering at them from the canyon wall, reaching out for the paint's bridle.

The shot had no effect that Lee could see in that instant and, in the rolling, jolting commotion of his hanging ride, he stretched the Colt's out under the horse's neck again and fired another shot, this directly into the reaching giant's chest as he put out his arm to grip the paint's leathers.

That shot surely must have killed the big man, because he did not grasp the paint's bridle and haul him to a stop. The *cabron* is a dead one, Lee thought, and was just hauling himself back up into the saddle (had spurred the pinto hard as he did to keep it galloping full out), was just barely set up in the saddle, when a rifle shot came cracking across the gully floor, struck the little paint, and killed it in mid-stride.

Lee stood, shaking out of the stirrups as

the paint folded under him, its legs still pumping, hooves ringing on stone, its powerful, slab-sided muscles still racking in its run. Doing all this, though, it still folded, sank, collapsed, and finally struck the streaking dirt with its nose, its neck and chest and slid, already dead, a long, rough, noisy slide along the stones.

Lee parted company, and went sailing quite a way beyond.

He tried to stay upright, windmilling through the air, feet running on nothing, but could not do so. The moment one boot sole struck the earth, so did he, and very hard, was rolled and beaten and skinned along the ground.

He kept the Colt's in his hand, and was saved by doing it, because a thin man came running up the *arroyo* toward him as he lay in a heap, frosted with yellow dust, small bright purple dots revolving and revolving in his sight. He could see the canyon dirt and rock beyond them, but the purple dots continued to revolve, though they grew small as Lee managed to sit up.

He saw the thin man—dark skinned, heavily oiled black hair worn long as a woman's . . . a handsome, clever face. Or would have been handsome with the addition of a few of his previous teeth. Fellow was grinning, happy as a hog at trough, coming at Lee with a single-barreled shotgun and now just stopping his run to catch his breath and aim it.

Lee lifted his right hand and fired before he thought to do it, before he'd noticed he still had the hand-gun in his grasp. The Colt's might have done his thinking for him.

That shot missed, but made the thin man wince before he set himself again to level on Lee and kill him. This flinching cost the man his life.

Lee rose up onto his right elbow, stared hard at the fellow's belly covered in torn, stained-cotton trousers and shot him there.

At first, Lee thought the man'd exploded from the injury; then he realized it had been the shotgun going off wild. The bits of shot went humming off across the gulch in a quick sort of swarming. Lee thumbed the hammer on the Bisley Colt's, and shot the thin man again. The fellow was staggering this way and that, crooning, gripping his red-soaked trousers with red and delicate hands.

This second shot knocked the man off his feet and he lay in the bright yellow dust on his side, his legs making slow walking motions.

As that thin bandit went down, Lee got up, stood still for a moment, testing whether he had broken any bones—and ducked as another rifle shot came buzzing past him to smack into the gully wall a dozen yards past. The round had missed Lee by very little.

The new Winchester was still in its scabbard with the pinto.

Lee lit out running, heading back to the heap of dead horse—that nasty little paint, that sturdy, vicious kicker. It had carried him down out of the Oregon Territory, out of a certain small town up there where two men had been shot to death. Had carried him, later, out of an even smaller town in northern California, where a sawmill payroll had been looted at gunpoint, a constable killed.

Lee lowered his head as though he were running in a rain, and galloping along for his life. Knew he must look ridiculous to the man or men who watched him from the *barranca's* other side. He had seen men run for their lives. No dignity. No dignity in that.

The few yards to the horse's body seemed a British mile. Lee was almost there when he felt he was sighted down. He *knew* it.

He fell flat as though shot already and the round came clipping through the air above him, snapping past with a personal sound.

Lee twisted up, hoping for a glimpse—the son-of-a-bitch must be up high—and caught more than that, saw the man as big as life standing at the gully's opposite rim, some thirty or more feet up outlined in a blaze of sunlight, aiming his rifle again.

Lee raised the Colt's and fired at the fellow. No effect at that range, of course, near two-hundred yards. He heaved up onto his feet again, fired another shot for theatrics, and dove for the paint and his rifle.

The little horse had fallen and rolled to his right side. Inconvenient. Lee, feeling skinned knees and an aching elbow—hurt enough to be near busted—for the first time since his fall, scooted around to that side of the animal and commenced to wrench at the rifle stock protruding from under the dead beast's shoulder.

Hard tugging.

The man on the rim fired again. Lee didn't know where the bullet went, but not into him, thank God. No question, though, that he was a dead *gringo* if he didn't get the Winchester clear and working. Such a fine piece, too. Beat the old Henry all hollow . . .

Lee sat down in the dirt as another rifle slug came at him—knew where *that* one went; it slammed into the dead pinto's haunch. Didn't shift him but might as well have, since it gave Lee sufficient encouragement to grip the end of the Winchester's stock near hard enough to dent the walnut, set his boots up against the horse's body, and heave for all he was worth and then some. Would be surprised if the rifleman (and friend or friends) weren't laughing hard enough at this spectacle (Don Luis' ferocious Yankee *pistolero* trying to pry his rifle from under a dead horse) to spoil their aim.

Lee devoutly hoped so, anticipated the next rifle round and pulled even harder at the Winchester's stock. The rifle came suddenly sliding free from under the pinto's bulk and Lee threw himself back and away as the next rifle shot popped past his ear.

He rolled onto his belly—no time to scramble around to the horse's lee side—levered the Winchester (difficult to imagine a sweeter sound in a tight) and leveled it at the *barranca's* rim.

The fellow there was something of a slow-top, it appeared. He must have seen Lee haul his rifle free but he seemed to pay no heed to it. Still stood upright as a lead soldier, and as Lee brought the Winchester's sights down upon him, stepped from the gully rim and commenced a slow, awkward, sliding descent, his rifle held in one hand as he did it.

Hard to say why a man will do such a foolish thing in a fight. The constable at Russian River had done just such a foolish thing as Lee came walking out of the saw-mill shed on a pitch black night, leaving three men (two guards and a clerk) hog-tied and gagged behind him. The gagging and tying of one had been superfluous—a gunman and guard named Ike Perry had objected to the robbery, and Lee had had to beat him unconscious. The constable, a young man named McManus, had surprised Lee there in the dark, and had thrown the light of a lantern upon him, while naming him arrested. Some stray mill-hand must have seen or heard the action in the office, and run to fetch this young law-bird.

McManus had accosted Lee, called him to account and thrown the light of a lantern on him. Lee had instantly fired into that light and struck McManus in his chest and killed him. The foolish man had been holding the lantern directly in front of him.

So, a first-time robber—a sort of romantic highwayman he might be regarded, if one were not too particular—had become a law-shooter. A police-killer.

A fugitive into this warm land of Mexico.

Lee got his bead . . . held it—what in hell was the man climbing down for?—then squeezed off his round.

No puff of rock dust anywhere around the fellow. A certain hit, though the man didn't show it. Kept that awkward slow scramble down the *barranca* wall, rifle still held up and out of the way of stone-scrapes or scratches . . .

Lee levered and shot the man again.

This round, at least, made a considerable impression. The bandit, who appeared to be a tall, well set-up fellow, a *serape* still neatly draped across one shoulder, suddenly threw up his hands, as if Lee's rifle had called for such a surrender, threw them up and commenced a slow turn, like a show-off at a *baile,* then slowly toppled forward off the wall's low face. He fell past twenty feet of rock wall and landed, as near as Lee could tell, directly on his head. Man had held his rifle all the way down.

There, by God! Pack of damned greasers, to run an attempt on Don Luis' Yankee!

Lee looked over his shoulder to see if the other two were still down. Further along the *arroyo,* the thin one with oiled hair had stopped his walking lying down. Looked dead as mutton.

Back a ways, Lee saw that the big one who'd tried for the paint's reins was not down and dead.

That fellow, a first bullet in him somewhere, a second surely in his chest, was up and about after a fashion. Crawling up the gulch as if going for help . . . as if help might be found out there, in the fry-pan heat, the nests of scorpions, rattlesnakes, cactus spines.

Lee had an opportunity then, for one of those cruely comic shots that will occur in a long and complicated fight. The big man's large buttocks presented themselves as he crawled slowly away, each cheek shifting massively under its trouser seat of dirty white cotton. A bull's eye for sure.

Plenty of men would have taken that shot, laughing.

Lee shot the big man through his left thigh and, as he toppled and rolled half over, levered again and took him very neatly with a second, just over his crotch and belly, and through his head.

Crisp shooting, and satisfactory.

Lee levered the Winchester again for fresh—and the weapon jammed.

No surprise—Mexican re-loads into used brass. Had sworn he'd go to Del Suberio for *Yanqui* ammunition, and had not troubled to do so. No surprise and his fault, not the Winchester's. Lee knelt up to clear it—the cartridge had caught half-ejected—and a man came running at him from near where the fool with the rifle had fallen. This man was short, and thick through the shoulders, but he seemed at the distance to have a face at odds with his body, a thin, big-nosed bird's face. He wore crossed bandoliers—a sign of leadership among bandits—and he fired a large revolver at Lee, once, and then again as he came running. He also shouted something but Lee couldn't make it out.

Lee didn't think. He dropped the jammed Winchester, drew his Colt's, flipped the gate, dropped one empty out into the sand, pulled a fresh round from his belt, thumbed it into the cylinder, eased the hammer, spun the cylinder, pulled the hammer back, swung the piece up and aiming, and slipped the hammer to fire. The live cartridge had spun to where it should be. The Colt's went off.

The slug struck the shouting man in his chest, broke his shout off in a grunt, and a bone there in a quick crack as the lead went through.

The bandit leader glared at Lee as if he could, by staring dreadfully enough, kill him. He stumbled to a stop no more than ten feet away and carefully lifted his revolver—an old Smith and Wesson Russian .44, Lee saw—to put this bullet where he wished it. And looked steady enough to get it done.

Lee scrambled to his feet like a kicked dog. He took a great stomping leap to the left, spun on his heel, and dove to the right, reaching down into his right boot-top as he did. He rolled, and came to his feet just as the Smith and Wesson went off with a considerable bang. Lee felt a sting at the inside of his left knee—could still stand—palmed the broad-blade dagger in his right hand, drew that hand back like a baseball pitcher, and threw the knife spinning.

The bandit saw it coming. Lee saw the flicker of his eyes, but the man was too badly hurt to go tumbling over the countryside as Lee had for the dodge. He stood stock still (dying, no doubt, from that shot to his chest) and fired the Smith and Wesson as the dagger whacked into his belly—nine inches of broad, double-edge steel—and left him doubled over on his knees, his big revolver fallen into the sand beside him, of no use at all.

Lee stood beside the dead paint, and his hands trembled for a moment as though he had a chill . . . as though he were in the mountains to the east on one of the cold nights there . . .

This weakness in his hands had happened before a time or two, and always after a serious fight. There was no difficulty about it. The fight was always over when the trembling came and it didn't last long.

He walked over to the kneeling man. The bandit *jefe*—a small chieftain, surely, to command only three men—was doubled over hard, his bloody hands clenched on the dagger handle almost concealed in the billow of his dirty shirt. The leather bandoliers looked too heavy for the man as he crouched there.

"¿Que tal, hombre?"

But the kneeling man had no answer to make, except to slowly shake his head as if in comment on Lee's stupidity in asking. The man shook his head and gripped the handle of Lee's knife as if he were afraid the blade would slide out and escape him. Surprising the fellow was still alive, with a bullet through his chest as well. Perhaps not so surprising. In his year and a half in Mexico, besides finding himself oddly adept at learning Spanish (Lee'd been all the more startled by this knack since he'd had no call even to try another tongue, unless Professor Riles' Latin could be counted) Lee had also learned that the Mexican people possessed a particular toughness, a bitter sort of endurance that had little to do with what an *Americano* regarded as hardihood. They were an enduring people, silent, merry, and cruel. Lee had grown very fond of them and had learned from them.

It seemed to him now that it would be unpleasant, for some reason, to go about the business of reloading his revolver in order to fire it into this *bandito's* head. No more pleasant to reach under him and wrench the knife handle from his grip so that Lee might cut his throat.

Simplest was best, it seemed.

Lee looked about him, saw and dismissed a small rounded stone, then saw a larger one, a rock with an angle to it. He walked over, picked it up, walked back.

"*Vaya con Dios,*" he said, raised the rock in both hands, and brought it smartly down onto the back of the fellow's head. The blow made a dull cracking sound, not as loud as Lee expected, and laid the man out flat. Lee stood over him, his hands stinging from the force of the first blow, and struck at the fallen man's head again.

This time the bone broke thoroughly, and as if in approbation the corpse loosed a long tootling fart.

Chapter 2

Lee found their horses, four dreary little saddle-galled scrubs, at the far south end of the *barranca* rim. His little paint would have made two of any of them. A horse to be missed, that nasty little kicker. Had saved Lee's life, once, kicking.

Lee unhobbled two of the scrubs and let them drift away. The better two he led back down into the arroyo. No one of the animals would be able to carry him, his stock saddle, his war-bag and rifle, his *Saltillo* blanket roll, and the saddle-bags with the silver.

Have to be ride one, pack the other.

And so he did.

The land rising up into the *Porcupinos* was dry as a dead cow's skull, dotted with *maguey* and cactus. It humped itself slowly up in broad shelf after shelf, ridge after ridge, like a great brown beast rising from a long sleep under the broiling sun.

It was big country, and beautiful in its way, but there was no shade, no ease at all in it. It was country indifferent to what human or horse might come crawling over it. It cared nothing for them.

Four kites were circling high, tiny black crucifixes swinging against an endless blue-white bowl of sky. And even here in the wilderness, Lee could faintly smell the scents of Mexico drifting in the breathless, baking air. Human shit was there . . . always present, even in the corridors of Don Luis' great *hacienda*, even in the governor's palace at *Hermosillo;* the scent of dung, if not its actuality. That, then, and half-tanned leather, and sugar cane drinks all the colors of the rainbow. Spilled beer, and marijuana smoke.

All the stinks of greaserdom, a North American might say, and be dead right.

Lee had grown to enjoy them. They spoke of life, stubborn and quarrelsome, still at its work in this fierce country. He had ridden down across the *Bravo* nearly two years before, had stopped at *Renosa* to drink and whore and rest and to take the measure of this Mexico. He'd liked it from the first and had not been troubled by the hatred many of these brown men felt for the white men of the north who had whipped them in two hard wars.

Lee had pretended to be nothing but what he was—a horse-raiser, a gunman, and now, a thief with a price on his head. He had also, much more important, swiftly learned Spanish (or at least a fluent sort of border variety of the language) and so had pleased many Mexicans who were too used to being shouted at by Americans who refused to try any language but their own.

In that way and not, for the time being, being handicapped by poverty, Lee had gotten on well enough, staying clear, when he could, of the other Yankee roughs who'd drifted south in preference to a sheriff's noose.

Had gotten on well, had enjoyed himself, had minded his own business . . . until a visit from an agent of the local *policia.* This small man, named Rosario y Vega, had come to the Florita one morning; found Lee in his room, and sat down on Lee's only chair for a small conversation.

It appeared that the Federal marshal of the Territory of Northern California had made certain approaches to the Captain— one Edgar Swaine—of the Texas Ranger Post in McAllen, concerning a fugitive wanted in connection with the slaying of an officer of the law . . . a certain constable.

This same Captain Swaine, a fierce man,

very bold, and not particularly a respecter of borders and boundaries, had made peremptory demands of the police in Renosa to produce this fugitive.

So, Rosario y Vega, *agento,* had come to the Florita on this cool, rainy morning—"And haven't we needed this rain? And who but the Sweet Virgin, and of course, his Excellency the Governor, could be praised for providing it."

Brought gently to the point (Lee had no wish at all to murder this little man, then to flee the Florita in a hustle and bustle headed God knew where) *Senor* y Vega, by and by, reckoned that a sturdy tale of death in the back country, supported by a very ripe corpse (there were, as it happened, two appropriate Yankees currently sick to death with the tar shits in the wards of the convent clinic even as he spoke) allowed perhaps to ripen for some days . . . properly clothed . . . found by the nuns to have this and that about him . . . a proper watch . . . proper papers . . .

Senor y Vega reckoned that such an exhibit might persuade even the Protestant Swaine that a bad man had gone to his certain punishment in Hell.

"It sounds an expensive exhibit," Lee had said in very creditable Spanish, and *Senor* y Vega had agreed sadly that that was so. A wonderful arrangement and an expensive one.

It cost Lee every penny he had taken out of the sawmill office safe, except for the sum of one hundred dollars. This last was allowed him because, as the chief of the Renosa police said, "Without it he will surely rob Mexicans, as he has already robbed his own."

This incident, which made armed stealing seem like a losing game indeed to Lee—though he wouldn't, it was true, have been harrassed over the border had not McManus been such a fool with that lantern—confirmed for him the necessity of finding some more acceptable employment, even if only slightly more acceptable.

"We would also desire you, at your convenience, to depart . . . to ride away from Renosa, if you could bring yourself to do so . . ."

"Much as that will pain me," Lee had answered the Chief of Police in his improving Spanish, "much as I will sorrow to be parted from such municipal loveliness . . . such civilization, I realize the necessity of doing so."

"Tomorrow?"

"My plan exactly."

"At least, a gentleman," the Chief said to *agento* Rosario y Vega, after Lee had bowed, shaking hands, and left the offices. "A cut above the usual Yankee *pistolero.*"

"A dog of breeding," said y Vega, and both men laughed and then went out to lunch, though usually they did not lunch together.

Thereafter, Lee, trusting that he was dead as possible to the American authorities—but not trusting that completely enough to wish an interview with Captain Swaine of the Texas Rangers—traveled west a long way, into Sonora. And was mighty pleased by it.

He rode there through a mountain range of stacked boulders, stones, pebbles, the like of which he'd never seen—and saw besides, huddled in each narrow mountain valley, a small *rancho* carpeted with grass as green as ever grew in Idaho Territory. That sweet grass . . . a small, sturdy *adobe* ranch house . . . running water (always a good year-round creek draining from the odd mountains rising at either side) and small herds of very respectable stock. Long-horned cattle . . . very good horses.

At these *ranchos*, he had stopped, not missing one, and had accepted his meal and night of hospitality, and asked for work in the morning.

Struck, perhaps, by the oddity of a *gringo* and a *malo,* obviously, requesting honest work, many of the *rancheros* had taken Lee on for a few days' work or a few weeks' work. They had, most of them, no more work than that to give, since their own people, living in tiny cabins on their land, had an hereditary right to what stock-chivvying or haying had to be done.

Still Lee worked and kept most of his hundred dollars safe in his purse.

He had serious trouble only once and that came from taking sides at a country *baille* against two brothers who threatened his *patron* of the week, a gentle work-worn man who leased his land and ran only seventy head of scrub cows on it.

This man, named Gaspar Molina, had offered Lee shelter and two meals of tortillas and beans a day to hold that small herd still on the banks of a creek called Chabectli, while Molina and his son went up into the mountains to round strays, there being no more than seven or eight of those.

Doing this small duty, Lee had held the cattle by the water—no difficult feat, since cinch grass was also growing just that high through the whole stretch of grazing—had held them for six days until Molina and his boy rode in happy with five of their strays.

Pitiful doings, this would have been called in the north . . . in the States. But Lee enjoyed it and liked both Molina and his boy, Toribio.

It was this man Molina that the two brothers Sanchez attempted to bully. Some question of winter graze back in the hills.

The Sanchez brothers—Lee never knew their Christian names—approached Molina as he and his boy were watching the dancing, and commenced to insult the man right there publicly, insulting the memory of Molina's wife, who had been from all Lee had heard a decent woman, though sickly.

Molina was no coward, but he was slow-witted and gentle; his boy like him as two peas. They weren't up to disputing.

The Sanchez brothers were odd bullies to see, being middle-aged with white in their hair, one shorter than the other with a sharper face. They were well dressed in wool and leather, had spent money on their clothes, and on hair oils and perfume. They each wore revolvers in *buscadero* holsters at their hips.

Lee had gone to get a sweet roll from a woman selling some, and was considering the courtesies of asking one of the Mexican girls to dance—he had his eye on a tall girl, very handsome, with a faint wine-colored birthmark at the corner of her lips. Looked as though she'd been eating strawberries.

He'd noticed the crowd gathered to listen to the baiting of the Molinas, and walked over there, munching the sweet roll.

Heard what one of the brothers was saying, over the heads of the crowd, and then pushed his way through to the front. Ordinarily, Lee would have stood wide of such a show, the Molinas' business being, after all, their business. Ordinarily, but not now.

He was a Molina hand, though for only tortillas and beans. A Molina hand, and would be till the hour he quit or was sent off. Lee behaved as he would have expected any of *his* hands to have behaved on Spade Bit. When you worked a place you were *of* the place or you weren't worth much.

". . . A fine pair," the taller of the Sanchez brothers was saying. "Thieves of grazing land today—who can say what will find its way into their pockets tomorrow! Perhaps some of your pigs, Olivero? We wouldn't be surprised by that. A family of pigs . . . what could be more natural than their gathering more pigs to themselves?"

Some awkward laughter at that sally.

"The mother of this Molina son . . ." the other brother chimed in like a hallway clock.

"*Silencio!* With your permission, Patron." Lee stepped clear of a man beside him, crowding his gun arm. "I say, be silent," Lee said to the Sanchez brothers. "The only pigs I see here are imitating human speech, and poorly."

"By the Saints! This damn *gringo* barks like the Molinas' dog!" The taller Sanchez put his hand on the butt of his revolver. "You Texas thing," he said to Lee, and started to say something more, but Lee had no intention of letting him run on, of letting this matter come to shooting.

Lee stepped one step forward and kicked the taller Sanchez in the stones.

That man, very badly hurt, stood frozen,

still gripping the butt of his holstered revolver but apparently in no condition to use the weapon.

Lee shoved the injured man aside so hard that he staggered and fell down and drew, cocked, and leveled the Bisley Colt's while the other Sanchez, barely decided, had his revolver only half out of the leather.

"Don't force me to kill you," Lee said, proud to have remembered his Spanish in such a pass.

Neither Sanchez looked to be forcing him to do any such thing, though the crowd about them seemed something disappointed at their tameness.

"Protestant!" the taller Sanchez said, sitting on the ground. His face was very pale from the pain of being kicked. He was keeping his right hand away from the butt of his revolver.

The other brother stood staring at Lee's Colt's as if the pistol had sprung into Lee's hand by witchcraft. This brother had nothing to say. He watched the muzzle of the Colt's.

"Please . . . please," Molina said, and put a worn and calloused hand on Lee's gun arm. "There is no need to harm them . . ."

"As you order, *Patron,*" Lee said, glad to be so easily out of it. "Should they insult the Molina land and the Molina name further however, it will be my pleasure, if you send for me, to return."

"No, no . . ." Molina said, as the shorter Sanchez, still keeping a wary eye on Lee's revolver muzzle, helped his wincing brother to his feet. "No, no . . . we have no need of violence here," the worn brown hand patting at Lee's arm as if Lee were some wild young stallion to be quieted.

There was considerable murmuring around them; an event of the first importance had apparently occurred in the pueblo with this fracas. A stranger *gringo* had, in Molina's name, humbled *both* of the Sanchez brothers. "Pride goeth before a fall" indeed. And this North American, with eyes the color of amber and a pistol so quickly obedient—there even seemed a possibility he was *El Cabrito,* Billy the Kid!

So that story began its silly round. The elder Molina inquired of him the next day as he was saddling the little paint. "If I am being rude, I beg you will tell me, *Senor.* Is it that you are Billy the Kid?"

"I am not," Lee told him, and saw that the *ranchero* was somewhat disappointed. "I have met him, however. He is bigger than ordinary men, and fierce as a puma."

"Truly? You met him?"

"Only once. A noble fellow, for all his fierceness."

With this lie, Molina was well pleased—to have met a man who had met that legendary defender and friend to the Mexican people in distant *Nuevo Mexico.*

Lee had had no heart to tell him that the Kid, a small Brooklyn hoodlum with buck teeth, and by all accounts mean as a snake, had been shot to death in a dark room by a panicked Patrick Garrett.

Lee'd bade the pleased Molina farewell, leaned down to shake Molina's boy by the hand, and spurred the little paint on out to start the long switch-back climb up the next narrow range of pebbly mountains. Was a hot day, but with a breeze—not bad for riding.

That was the only trouble he'd seen so far in Mexico—and had, after all, been nothing for a man to preen himself on—to have cowed two blustering old *rancheros*. Not precisely a hero's deed . . .

A month or a little more later, Lee had ridden down into the valley of the Rio Matape, and seen La Colorado. The pueblo stretched along the river bank for a quarter of a mile, white-walled, red-roofed in the dazzling sunlight. A light green haze of cottonwoods ran along the river's course, and backed the town like a curtain, cool and verdant.

It was a small settlement . . . peaceful.

Lee had ridden into La Colorado's cobble-stoned streets at *siesta* time, the paint's hooves ringing on the rock. There was otherwise no sound at all about the town except for a woman singing far down the street and a distant noise of crows in the fields beyond.

The town was asleep and Lee, deciding to join it, rode down a jacaranda-blossomed alley to the grassy river bank, pulled the pinto up, unsaddled him, hobbled him, and left him, ass high, sucking water from a glassy, shallowy eddy of the stream. Lee walked back up higher on the bank, found a deep shifting patch of shade beneath a very old cottonwood, lay down, hitched his gun-belt more comfortable, tucked his crumpled Stetson beneath his head, and drifted to sleep as if he drifted on the waters of the Metape.

Lee lived in La Colorado for three months, made some money working for Geronimo Gayana, the smith in the town, and made some friends as well.

Then one morning, on the fourth of August, two deserters from the *Rurale* station at Empalme rode drunk up the river and, stopping at La Colorado to refresh themselves, broke into the back of Pedro Alvarado's dry goods store to rob it. While there, they stabbed Alvarado and his wife to death; then, apparently repenting of their haste, stripped the woman's corpse and raped it.

The whole street had of course heard the Alvarados' screams, but they had also seen

that the men who were the occasion of that
noise and who had kicked the store's door
off its hinges to enter, were dressed in the
grey-blue jackets, the silver buttons and
facings of the *Rurales*. So the people of that
street had listened to the screams but had
left their own weapons, their *machetes*,
their hoes, their ancient muskets, undis-
turbed. They had gone to their houses and
stayed there.

When those two men came out of the
Alvarados' store, one still fastening up his
trousers, and both spattered here and there
with blood, Lee had been standing by the
town fountain—a very handsome fountain,
with a carving of an eagle on top of the
stone—with his Winchester rifle in his
hands.

It was a puzzle to the townspeople after-
ward why he had interfered at all, the
Alvarados not being special friends of his.
It was thought possible that *Senora*
Alvarado's screams had worked to irritate
nerves unaccustomed to such sounds. It
was well known that Yankees of all sorts
were somewhat spoiled with soft living, and
had no notion of fate at all . . .

The two men, owlish drunk, had barely
time to recognize that some difficulty
impended before one was shot through the
head like a duck. The other, he who was
buttoning his clothes, was shot thereafter
through the body, fired back with his

revolver, and then was shot again, the bullet carrying a piece of his intestine away.

And no sooner had the gunsmoke drifted off than, just as in a play at the theater in Hermosillo, a troop of *Rurales*, hanging ropes at their saddle cantles, came galloping into the square, searching for their deserters. The *Rurales* had a short way with deserters.

A North American might have expected the Lieutenant of *Rurales* to be pleased that his business had been done for him, even if by a *gringo*. A citizen of Mexico would have known better.

It took some talk by the *Alcalde* and other men of the town to prevent the Lieutenant from ordering Lee strung up in the deserters' place.

It took some talk, but the talk had prevailed.

A week later, a *vaquero* rode into town. He was a rider from Las Sabrinas, and Las Sabrinas was the land, the country, the hills, the great Rancho to the north. All—and much more than that—was the property, the kingdom, of Don Luis Arturo Ortiz-Cordoba de Spania.

It was this kingly man, as powerful, almost, as the Governer himself, who wished to see the *norteamericano*, Lee McCann. (Lee had felt "McCann" to be a reasonable substitute for a name Captain Swaine of the Texas Rangers would be almost certain to notice, should it accidently be brought to his attention north of the border. "Lee Morgan" was a bit too famous a fellow.)

Lee, on the advice of the townspeople, had packed up his war-bag, saddled the paint, and followed after the *vaquero*, meek as a sheep, to go and kow-tow before this Mexican Grandee. It had seemed a wise vacation in any case, as long as the troop of *Rurales* stayed quartered in the town. Their Lieutenant gave Lee hard looks every time their paths crossed, and their paths looked to cross often if Lee remained for the while in La Colorado.

The *vaquero*—his only given name Vincente, as far as Lee could tell—was an elderly man, gnarled and dark and twisted as a root. He was silent as a root, too, and occasionally reminded Lee of his foreman, Ford. Ford was something younger, of course, and white. But there was the same reclusive toughness, silence, about both men. And for all his age and the age of his horse, a long-toothed grey named *Rosinante*, the old man kept the lead with no apparent effort in the five long days it took them to arrive at Las Sabrinas.

They rode the ridges of the hills bordering the Matape, rode them the hot days through. Then, in the evenings, they walked their horses down the slopes to the river . . . camped there, fished (the old man an expert with hook and line) cooked the fish over mesquite twigs, smoked vile corn-husk cigarettes, looked at each other occasionally, went off into the brush to do their individual necessities, returned to the fire, smoked other cigarettes, and went to sleep to the music of the river and the soft, murderous, high-pitched cries of the owls that flew through the cottonwoods, hunting.

Lee woke in the middle of the first night, saw that the old man was not in his blankets, picked up his Winchester and walked out to find him.

Vincente was standing by a lightning-killed water oak, on watch, his old Spenser cradled in his arms. Lee came up to him, motioned with his thumb for the old man to return to his blankets, and took his place.

In that way, the two of them came to their agreements about standing guard. Over the next few days of traveling, their agreements grew to cover all trailing matters. Still, the old man hardly spoke at all, and whenever Lee essayed his not-too-awkward Spanish, would look at him in apparent astonishment, as if he expected that *gringos* had hardly been gifted with speech at all—much as if Lee had been a cattle-dog, and had suddenly remarked upon the weather.

In this fashion they traveled, and did well enough, and rode always higher along the

river's course, higher into ever greener
country. It was cattle country, now, or
horse-raising country. The grass, when Lee
leaned from the saddle to pluck up a long
yellow-green leaf of it to chew, had the salt-
stone taste of fine grazing. Sure enough, on
the morning of the fourth day, he saw the
first herd. Long-horned cattle, as Molina's
had been, but bigger, fine, and fat, and
branded with a large and simple "S."
Sabrinas. It appeared to Lee an easy brand
to imitate, and he wondered how this rich
Don kept his beeves from being stolen from
him. Any Idaho rustler—even any Texican
rustler—would have made the finest "S"
seen with a few strokes of a running iron,
and been a small rancher in a jiffy.

The costs of this sort of enterprise,
however, Lee saw to be high on midday
next.

He and Vincente were riding a track—
very nearly a road, it was, well carved by
wagon wheels—when they came upon a
large sign erected on two strong, tall poles.
LAS SABRINAS. The letters had been
burned deep into the wood.

At either end of the long sign, a naked
man hung by his heels, swollen and dead—
dead, evidently, simply from hanging for a
considerable time upside town. The great
Sabrinas "S" had been branded deep in
each man's bare belly.

Perhaps not so easy and safe to use a

running iron in this country after all. Likely
not.

Lee had no notion that this sign represented the beginning marker of Don Luis
Arturo Ortiz-Cordoba de Spania's ranch-
land. He knew, had known from the way the
old vaquero sat his saddle, that Vincente
had been riding home grass for two days.
This marker simply stated the commence-
ment of a yard or perhaps, a lawn leading to
the man's home itself.

Lee guessed that home to be another
day's ride to go.

He was right.

Chapter 3

At dawn of the sixth day, Vincente had risen, gone to piss, come back to camp—they'd slept under chaparral along the brow of a hill—and had announced simply, "Las Sabrinas."

There was no second gateway . . . no sign or cairn or marker of any sort. Only the track grew more traveled, deeper scarred by wagons and horses' hooves.

Lee and the old man rode the track all the morning, over slowly rising hills and breaks thick with sedge and broom-grass. Birds flew up beside their horses, and cloud shadows flowed over the hills like floods of shade, and drifted on.

It was handsome country, and it made Lee ache to ride over it. He felt at times that he might lift his head to see the Rocky

Mountains rising to the west . . . to hear the shouts of his men chivvying horses down the hills . . .

They saw only two other riders that morning. Two *vaqueros* sat their mounts on a distant rise, watching them, and did not move to answer old Vincente's wave. The two horsemen watched Lee and the old man for a few minutes, then turned their horses' heads and rode away.

. Just before noon, by Lee's fine silver-backed repeater watch won in a poker game in Amarillo, they came upon the house . . . not a house, really, rather a collection of dazzling white adobe buildings, several two stories tall, that clustered around a central walled yard big enough to play a game of baseball in.

More like a village than ranch-house.

And it grew bigger as Lee and the old man rode toward it.

The old man left Lee at a black wrought iron gate, then led the horses away. The gate was let into a low snow white adobe wall compassing a wide yard of combed and raked yellow gravel. Eight lemon trees, equally spaced, fronted the house beyond.

Lee looked at the house for a while— looked as much like one of the Spanish mission churches as a house—then leaned at his ease against the gate, lit one of the dreadful corn-husk cigarettes (longing considerably for a Havana cigar, rum-dipped), and baking like a lizard in the heat.

After a while, a big woman dressed in black came waddling down the walk, opened the gate, and motioned Lee to follow.

The house was cool as the day was hot. Cool, and very large, with glistening black hardwood floors, black oak and leather furnishings looking old as sin . . . high walls white as laundered sheets, and hung with paintings too old to read as to detail, or tell the original colors of.

Lee waited for some time in the entrance hall. Then a fat old man in black trousers and a long white shirt came slippering along to beckon him to follow. Lee trailed this fat old fellow through other hallways and waiting-rooms as well until led to tall double doors, black as the polished floor.

The servant tapped on one of these, and a young voice called in English, *"Come in!"*

Don Luis de Spania was unexpected. Lee had anticipated some tall hawk-nosed old hidalgo, proud as Lucifer and as grasping.

"Come in, please, Mister McCann—it is 'McCann,' is it not?"

Don Luis de Spania was Lee's age, or a little older, short, broad-shouldered and broad-faced as a peasant, with teeth discolored from smoking and eyes as round, sharp, merciless and black as a magpie's.

Lee suspected he had been right, at least as concerned the "grasping."

"It's McCann at present, *Senor.*" Only after he'd spoken did Lee realize he'd spoken in Spanish. That habit had grown on him.

The Don threw back his head and laughed. "At present! I do like a man with a sense of humor! And a man so quick to learn a civilized language—and not too badly, though your accent smacks of Texas." The broad-shouldered man opened a small silver box on his desk, reached in, took out a cigar, and stood to walk around the desk to offer it to Lee. The Don limped, and very badly.

"A fall from a horse some years ago," he said, seeing Lee's glance at his legs. "Entirely my fault. The horse, an animal named Lagrimas, was perfectly splendid. I was an . . . imperfect rider."

Lee had been impressed by the days of land he had ridden to get here and impressed by the house and its compound, the power and wealth both represented. But he had seen fine houses before and great stretches of country owned by one man (had, in fact, owned a great deal of that commodity himself), and nothing of Las Sabrinas so impressed him as the Don's admission of poor horsemanship. He had known few men who would concede to that, and none of them had been rich and powerful.

There was more to Don Luis than his acreage.

He had another trick, too. The knack of knowing what a man wanted.

Lee took the cigar—a Jamaican and a beauty—pulled a Lucifer from his jacket pocket, and set the cigar tip to glowing.

The Mexican returned to his desk chair, limping deep as a woman with an aching hip. He sat down with a sigh, leaning back into fine Cordovan leather . . . carved walnut. He was dressed like a gentleman of the town in a dark gray suit. No putting on the *charro*, it seemed.

"Don't credit me with second sight in seeing you needed some good tobacco, Mister McCann. I watched you from this window . . . saw the face you made, puffing on your cigarette. Our Mexican tobacco is, I believe, second only to the French in vileness."

Lee drew on the cigar, saw an armchair near the Don's desk, and went and sat down in it without being asked. He felt he had stood and been impressed long enough. And as he sat, he was interested to see the slightest flicker of displeasure in the Don's bright black eyes.

"You're quite right," the Mexican said, and reached to take a cigar of his own from the silver box, "I am not really used to Republican ways . . . Too accustomed to the more punctilious manners of my countrymen." He lit his cigar, leaned back again to puff upon it and look carefully at Lee. "Please do have a seat."

They smoked their cigars at each other for a little while.

"I am considering," the Don said, after this while, "I am considering employing you—or asking if you *wish* to be employed, as a general factotum, an *executor* . . . an iron fist, you might say, in my velvet glove."

Lee took a bit of tobacco off the tip of his tongue. "Why choose me for such an offer?"

"For two reasons. First, as a stranger in this country . . ." He smiled. "Though one who speaks our language quite well—you would have few allegiances and would be allowed few, except to whichever considerable man employed you. And second, because you, far more than most fugitive North Americans, bring some special qualities to your employment."

"The shooting of *Rurales*?"

"Oh, that skill is the least of those qualities. Mind you, Mister McCann—or is "Morgan" more comfortable?—mind you, I don't make light of your abilities with that revolver, nor, I understand, your abilities with any weapon. You, Lee—may I call you

Lee?—are the rarest of commodities, a killer born (and that, with your parentage, is hardly surprising). I'll be blunt and say I'd have hired your father, if time and fate had not prevented it. I always hire the best."

"And those are your 'special qualities?' "

Don Luis de Spania must have spent a busy week telegraphing or having an agent telegraph from Hermosillo to the States and must have very efficient people up there as well, to have learned so much in so short a time.

"Not at all," the broad-shouldered man said. "Nor do I mean to boast of my information, which can be bought by anyone who wishes so to spend money. The qualities I spoke of are those that come with the owning of great lands and the managing of those lands, and the livestock and the people concerned with them. I wish, in other words, to hire a *man,* (he used the Spanish *hombre)* and not a hoodlum, or a vicious boy who enjoys injuring."

"I doubt I wish to be hired," Lee said.

"Oh, I believe you will." The Mexican's cigar had gone out and he paused to re-light it. "I believe you will, out of sheer boredom if nothing else. Assisting a village blacksmith is well enough if you are a man without sense or without balls. I might also, if I thought it necesary, point out that a man who has killed three law officers— even if, in the case of those two at La

Colorado, quite justifiably—is likely to stand in need of a friend with influence. You are, after all, a guest in my country . . ."

Lee appreciated that Don Luis did not trouble to state the obverse: that a man in Lee's position, who had an influential enemy, would be in perilous case.

"Do you care to speak of wages?" he said, and Don Luis smiled.

"Ordinarily my man of business would deal with business," he said, "but in this matter, I will relieve *Senor* Obregon of the necessity. You will be paid two hundred and fifty silver pesos each month you remain in my service."

Lee was startled by the amount; it was twice the wages a top foreman would command—more than twice the wages. It meant that the Don expected no naysaying. It meant he expected results . . . however.

Lee sat still, thinking about it. He might, he supposed, ride out of Sonora Province, ride far away, perhaps further south, to the jungle country, and let this pleasant, rich, and powerful Don find another man to do his shadow work. Lee might do that. And would surely find another such person in a few weeks . . . or months. It would not be possible to spend years assisting blacksmiths in the pueblos of Mexico. And even if it were possible to drown his life in such a way, he would end with nothing for it, not even the hope of getting back to the States again, back to the high country.

Don Luis was waiting patiently, sitting back at ease, watching the light blue smoke from his cigar coil slowly toward the room's vaulted ceiling.

"I'll take the job," Lee said. "And I'll do it for a year."

"Done!" said the Don, and he sat up straight, and held his hand out for Lee to shake. "You are of Las Sabrinas now!"

"Of Las Sabrinas . . ."

True enough.

Lee left Don Luis' study and entered a world all its own, a place separate from the common usages of men and women, a place where the Don, the Don's property, the Don's people all formed a community as richly self-involved as any bee-hive in mid-summer.

This was not perfectly strange to Lee. Any rancher, any great proprieter knew something of that working, living, breathing creature formed by any great single enterprise, any grand business upon the land.

Las Sabrinas enveloped him, took him to its bosom, made him its child.

Lee was led to the ranch store, where his worn trousers, ragged shirts, battered Stetson, cracked boots all disappeared and were replaced, for nothing but his initials on a paper chit, with fine grey wool charro trousers (two pairs), flannel shirts in grey, light blue, and dun, underthings of white cotton, wool socks, a Vera Cruz *sombrero*, dark grey, with a high, creased crown and wide, deep-curled brim. The new boots were a lengthier matter. The store keeper, a lively young sissy with oiled Burnsides, informed him that once his measurements were taken, it would be a matter of overnight before delivery of the new boots.

"Then I'll take the old ones back, until."

Impossible. Absolutely impossible. New men were given new clothes.

This was, Lee assumed, something like enlistment in an army, and he resigned himself to whatever foolishness Las Sabrinas required in order to make him one of its children. Better a few hours barefoot—a Mexican habit in any case—than to set about beating a sissy and searching the store for his old boots.

It was barefoot, then, but otherwise splendidly clothed (the ranch seamstresses did work above the ordinary) that Lee sallied out of the store room to the bathhouse, where two dull-faced *mojos* stripped and plunged him, soaped and scrubbed him. Then toweled him dry. Glad enough, after all, to be shut of a week's trail dirt.

Old Vincente was waiting for him at the bath-house door, nodding something more familiar than he had in all those days of riding—apparently considering Lee more of

the family—and took him away out of the
stable building where the bath-house and
laundry were located and off across another
wide, gravelled yard to what seemed a
bunkhouse row, and more particularly, to
the last section of that row, a low-ceilinged
room, puncheon floored, holding a wide bed-
stead, a dresser of drawers, a mirror and
washstand, and (an oddity) a small book-
case with, it proved, copies of Fenimore
Cooper, Shakespeare, Hawthorne and
Charles Dickens—all, Lee was relieved to
discover, in English editions. A neat
enough courtesy, and the Don's doing, no
doubt. Speaking a fair Spanish was one
thing, reading it another.

Vincente, from the doorway, crooked a
gnarled thumb into this chamber, stepped
back, inclined his head the slightest bit,
turned and walked away.

Lee was home.

For now.

The two little nags were near foundered
before Lee was half the distance to Paso
Robles.

Whatever the bandits had been, they had
not been two things—good shots, and wise
about horses. These saddle-galled little
beasts weren't fit to carry a child, let alone
a grown man, baggage, and silver.

Lee, at the base of a lengthy rise with yet
another rise beyond, pulled his horse up,

heard the led beast shuffle to a stop, and swung down out of the saddle. Walking time, unless he cared to end up carrying all his goods afoot. Once on the ground, though, he had another of those attacks of the trembles, as if the fight had been but minutes ago, rather than two and more hours past.

Hands trembled, skin started sweating up a cold rain of salt water, and something seemed stuck in his throat. He walked a little way off, to be more by himself, away from the shifting horses. Walked over there, near a stunted *cholla*, bent, his hands on his knees, retched, and vomited nothing much at considerable cost of discomfort.

Spat that out, drew a deep breath, went back to the horses and picked up the reins to lead. It would be a long climb to the top of the pass. He missed the small paint already, had missed him from the instant he died. Lost a friend there—a stupid one, perhaps, but a friend nevertheless. Animal had tried to kick him only once, had never tried to bite him at all; more than could be said for the mule Lee had given in partial trade. That creature would have bitten the balls off Jesus Christ.

The nags balked at the slope, though it was slight enough, and Lee, a foul taste of nerves or cowardice or whatever still in his mouth despite three long pulls at the canteen, had to lean down nearly to the ground to haul the lead along. Early evening, and the sand and rock under his boots still glowed with heat, the air still shimmered with it.

A long haul. Several times before he reached the crest of the pass Lee was tempted to swing up into the saddle and let the damn rack-of-bones founder, stagger, and die, just to teach him a lesson. As it was, in the considerable climb Lee was afforded the opportunity of stomping on two scorpions, an opportunity he took advantage of, and another of doing some harm to a small, sand-colored rattlesnake, an opportunity he let pass.

At the crest there was at last some sort of breeze, and Lee seemed to have sweated out the last of the four *banditos*. No question they had asked for killing as persistently as men could—had asked for it, and gotten it. It was also true that those men had known about the silver and shouldn't have. Some Las Sabrinas hand, or his woman, had talked when they ought to have kept their mouths shut.

And this had had to happen when Lee was making the run, not when the treasure cart and ten outriders was rolling on delivery every third week.

A special delivery for the Don. And, to be fair, more fighting than Lee usually saw in the Mexican's service. Don Luis hadn't lied when he'd said he wanted more than a killer. Delicate chores was what he'd had in mind. Delicate chores . . . and only a little bit of murder, here and there.

On the down-slope now, Lee hauled the lead nag in and swung up onto him. The little beast grunted and sagged at the weight, but Lee didn't give a damn; a three-mile uphill climb was walking enough!

Paso Robles was just visible far, far down the pass, guarding, as it had been sited to guard by the *conquistadors*, the entrance pass to the whole of northern Sonora.

Not much of a town, for all that. The *Banco National*, three *cantinas*, a few shops, numerous cattle-pens, and a railroad station visited once every two days by the *Especial* on its way to the coast. First class on that train was wood-slat benches stinking of piss and chicken feathers. Second class was for the cattle.

Delicate duties . . .

The first had been the persuading of Martin Torres.

Senor Torres was a decent fellow and a stubborn one. It was, the Don had explained, a matter of winter graze and water. There had been numerous attempts to point out to *Senor* Torres the foolishness of a small ranch owner being so greedy and unChristian as to deny his grass to those great proprieters, such as Don Luis himself, who had need of it during long drives to the north.

It was this stubborn and foolish man whom Lee was sent to reason with.

Lee rode north on the small paint—rode only at night, and rode fast. Torres had two strong sons, and Lee considered this as he rode. A man's sons were often the key to his purse as well as his heart.

Torres was a decent man and lived as a man, and not, as did many small ranchers, rather like an animal with cattle. He had a decent house rather than a wattle shed to live in, and had, besides, an out-house behind it. An amenity.

Lee arrived at *hacienda* Torres at dawn on the fifth day of riding and went to earth as deep as a fox. The paint was left up on the mountainside.

Lee lay in a ditch past the rancho's west pastures. Lay there through the day, the evening, and lay there still longer.

At moon-rise, other members of the Torres family having gone from their home out to the necessary house and then returned, *Senor* Torres himself, eschewing a latern, depending upon the moonlight, came out to relieve himself.

Lee met this decent man upon the path, struck him from behind, and dragged him away from his house, his loved ones, away from safety. Dragged the gasping man by moonlight out into the brush, and there woke the man, saw him recovered, and spoke to him.

"*Senor* Torres, are you well enough to listen to me?"

Torres had nodded, looking furious as a goaded bull through the mask of blood that striped his face. The blood was black in the moonlight.

"*Senor* Torres, I have been sent to murder your sons."

Not such a furious bull now. Beginning, perhaps, to be a frightened bull, and not for himself.

"I should prefer not to do so. My . . . employer . . . also hopes such measure will be unnecessary."

"I will not sell my land." The bull had found a source of courage. His land.

"But what is land without a son to leave it to?" Lee said. "It is only stones and dirt and empty of any other value to a man. Believe me when I say I'll kill your sons. Believe me also when I say I would regret it." Having said that, Lee struck Torres again, harder than he had before.

When Torres woke, his face bone-white here, blood-black there, Lee gently mopped at his injury with a bandanna.

"I struck you," Lee said, "so that you would listen more carefully to what I say to you. It is not, as it happens, a matter of *selling*. It might be a matter only . . . of *leasing* your land, say for ninety-nine years?"

Torres had begun to weep . . . possibly

from pain, possibly from a greater discomfort.

"Lease it, *Senor. Lease it.* You will not possess it then. Your sons will not possess it. But *their* sons will. Their sons' sons will possess the land again. Lease your land, *Senor,* and I will speak to my . . . employer. And then I will not have to kill your boys."

Lee had gotten up from the ground then, and left *Senor* Torres, a brave and decent man, sitting in the dirt. Lee left his bandanna with that *ranchero.* The cloth was caked with blood, and not worth taking away.

The Don had, at first, been less than pleased, but Lee had persuaded him that nearly a century's lease on that land was more wholesome for Las Sabrinas than a slaughtered *ranchero*, his slaughtered sons, and a daughter and widow still to be slaughtered.

"Very North American," said Don Luis later. "Very practical. I am not certain, however, that this sort of 'practicality' is most effective in dealing with our people. In future," he said, "do not substitute your judgment for mine, particularly if you are right."

The Don had not been joking. Lee had not thought for an instant that he was.

Chapter 4

Paso Robles was chilling now in the morning air, chilling with the approach of night after a day of frying. The bank would not be open till morning. Time now for a stable for the nags, a meal and a bed for Lee.

Perhaps, if the memory of four fools did not interfere, a girl at *Mamacita's*.

Lee didn't trouble to spur the bandit's horse down the cobbled strets of Paso Robles; he was content if the poor thing would keep staggering on to its stable. Have to sell the beast and its friend tomorrow. . . .

Tomorrow would also mark the last day of the year he had agreed to serve Don Luis. Something to think about. A man could play dog for only so long, then he stood in danger of becoming one . . .

Two small boys stood at the side of the steep street to watch Lee pass. He saw them staring at the worn little nag he was riding—staring at him, as well.

No people like the Mexicans for a nose for trouble. Well before Lee could have the bandit's horse stabled, well before he could have his first glass of *aguardiente*, Paso Robles would know that Don Luis' gringo *pistolero* had found trouble in bringing *something* (perhaps a sack of the Don's silver pesos) . . . had had trouble carrying some small cargo in his saddlebags.

And it was so.

Lee stood at the long bar in Mamacita's, content in a roar of noise, guitar music (which he had learned to care for; piano playing now sounded harsh and pounding to him, particularly when he had been drinking) the cracking sounds of boot-heels on the splintered flooring as vaqueros from two of the local ranches danced with the whores, told lies in loud voices, and occasionally glowered at their opposites from other brands, threatening knife-work if insulted.

It was a pleasant resort and not particularly a violent one. Lee had never seen a man killed at Mamacita's, though he had seen a fellow too drunk to defend himself have his eyes cut out by two bullies.

There were other *Norte Americanos* in the place. A drummer for some American barbed-wire company (Lee had seen him passing through before) and two roughs in Texican hats sitting in a corner, grinning at the whores and talking smut to any that passed their table.

As to the long bar, it was comfortably lined along both sides of him with serious drinkers, talkers, and thinkers, all with their drooping wide-brim sombreros pushed well back so as not to interfere with the lifting of glasses.

Beer was the tipple at Mamacita's for thirst, aquardiente and tequila for the rest. Lee had opted for beer and aquardiente, a large and very dirty glass of each—served to him, as it happened, by the owner of the joint—unless a short, sour man named Urube, who visited occasionally and was treated with considerable ceremony, was a part owner as well.

Mamacita (Luz Obregon) rarely worked the bar; that tall, dark brown, stork-like lady (her left eye white as milk) was usually found perched by her cash-box near the door. Her name, or nickname, was ironic, since anyone less the plump, amiable, motherly figure of Mexican womanhood would have been difficult to imagine. This "Mamacita" had no comfortable looks at all, no generosity whatsoever, and a tongue so poisonous the town priest crossed himself when they met.

Luz Obregon had asked Lee—had told him, in fact, when he first began riding to Paso Robles—that she would prefer he *not* make Mamacita's a regular watering hole. One-eyed Luz did not care for Yankees, even temporarily, and had no intention of having one as a regular customer.

This had all been said to him publicly—at the bar, in fact, and to a very interested audience. Lee had heard her out, agreed in his then still improving Spanish that she was quite right, and was showing the sort of social discrimination expected of the descendant of generations of Castillian ladies. Having said that, he had leaned far across the bar, and kissed the astonished (and very ugly) woman on the lips, declaring that unfortunately he was in love, and could not long bear to be away from her.

This event became a legendary one in the town, at least for a time, and Lee was regarded as a considerable curiosity, even for a gringo gunman.

It was felt at first that he was mad.

Later, it was decided that he was humorous—though perhaps mad as well.

At any event, The Kiss, as it became known, had had its effect, and though her manner to Lee did not change—still an elaborate demonstration of contempt

—there were those who claimed to see some rusty coquetry in it. And Lee was never denied entrance to Mamacita's.

It was this rail-thin woman, her good eye dark and constantly furious as a summer storm, who now slid another beer over the chipped cottonwood bar to Lee. She paused for a moment while he sipped it and smiled at her, then, with a disgusted snort, spun away to see to what degree the chuck-a-luck spinner was cheating the house.

Home.

Or, at least, a place as near a home as the bunkhouse room at Las Sabrinas . . . And other camps and shacks and whores' chambers.

Likely some sound along the bar, some voice raised toward the back of the room, reminded Lee of his men. Strange, with no folks alive at all—with Catherine Dowd dead, his father dead, his mother long since dead and gone. With Dowd, the little rich man, dead as well . . .

S'ien dead . . .

Strange that now, and more and more, it should be the faces of his men that haunted him, chased him through his dreams. Strange, since these not-much-more-than-ordinary cowpokers were certainly still alive and, if golden references could help them, had as good jobs in cattle and horse management as could be got. Strange that

that small bunch of horn-handed drovers, a bit handier with weapons than most of their kind, should stand so firmly in his memories.

Unfinished business, was what they seemed. Appeared to still be standing on the porch steps of headquarters house at Spade Bit, hearing him say the place was bust, hearing him say he was selling out to pay his debts.

"Hoof-and-mouth"—a nasty name for a nasty sickness. And the ruin of his horse herds, and their ruin the ruin of his land holdings, and their ruin, his. The men had stood, hats in hands, and listened to his talking. Ford . . . Sefton . . . Charlie Potts. . . Bud Bent, and two new-signed men who hardly counted.

They'd stood patiently on the porch steps and listened to him, listened to Lee trying on his dignity, trying to make the matter seem simply business. Simply business— and him dying of shame as he spoke to them.

Did die, he supposed, in a way. Certainly left a piece of himself fallen away on that porch, or in the lawyer's offices in Boise and Denver.

Somewhere along there, he had certainly lost a piece of himself. As if there was a chain hooked through his flesh, linked in some way, buried in, knotted to the land, the high mountain country at Spade Bit . . .

at Rifle River. The country his father and mother lay rotting in . . . the country S'ien lay rotting in.

Lee Morgan had ridden then, to anywhere, having left something behind him. His try in the Northwest, then a damned bungled robbery, then, Mexico.

How was he different from those two roughs at the corner table? He'd bathed more recently, was better dressed, had a master to serve. In these slight ways, and no others, was he different.

If his men had dreams of their own, of riding Spade Bit again, of riding Dowd-Leslie-Morgan land, they had better do as Lee had better do and boot those dreams out of their beds. There was no money to buy back two mountain ranches. Likely there would never be such money.

Lee finished his second beer, considered the bar—and felt the men on either side of him move slightly away.

It was a subtle thing. One moment, these two strangers had been siding him, drinking their drinks, talking with friends perhaps, perhaps only brooding on some woman, some luck, or some misfortune, and then they were gone. Oh, still standing at his side, but not so close.

The noise in Mamacita's had changed as well. Not quite as strident—slightly more subdued.

Lee eased back from the edge of the bar-counter, put down his beer, and looked up into Luz Obregon's cracked and fly-specked bar mirror.

Past his reflected shoulder, he saw a man standing facing him. Sergeant's stripes on a light blue uniform jacket.

Lee turned from the bar—not quickly— and noticed the men on either side of him stepping away, crowding back and no subtlety to it.

"You are wanted, gringo. Most immediately. Why he wishes to speak to such refuse is a question that only Capitan Gonsalves might answer."

This was said to Lee by a short, barrel-chested trooper of *Rurales,* a sergeant. A man Lee had seen before in Paso Robles but whose name he did not know. The sergeant had a strong Indian accent; Lee found it difficult for a moment to understand that last phrase about "refuse." Then he did. This sergeant was no charmer; he was one of those powerful, stocky men with a misleadingly fat face. Seeing only the face, a man might suppose the fellow to be no great shakes in a pickle. And would suppose wrong. Man looked like an overfed fighting dog, with a shade too much bull, a shade too little terrier in the breeding. He had clever eyes—very clever, for a sergeant.

Many of the *Rurales* had been recruited— as had, to be fair, many American lawmen—

from the general body of thugs, road-agents, and owlhooters whose tendency to violence made them so useful for that work. Lee sized the sergeant as just one such and clever enough to realize the *Rurales* made a more comfortable berth than a Mexican penitentiary or a hasty ditch beside a bullet-pocked wall.

"It is surely not that you are fool enough to be being rude to me, *Sergeanto!* Even though your low-born looks, so very Indian, would indicate it."

Spanish was a wonderful language of insult, particularly in its more intricate forms.

The sergeant flushed a darker brown, and one thick hand spidered slowly along his uniform belt toward his holstered pistol—a converted cap-and-ball, it looked, and slow as molasses in a high-fit holster.

Another trooper stood behind the sergeant. This one was taller, with that dreamy, introspective air so common in these people. Lee had decided long ago that Mexicans spent only a portion of their time considering the actual. They were dreamers to a man, though when they acted, they *acted.*

Lee didn't doubt the trooper with the carbine would be more trouble than the sergeant if it came to shooting.

Those neighboring had heard what the

sergeant had said, had heard what Lee had replied. This part of the room was very quiet now, though in the back they'd scarcely noticed. It took trouble indeed to silence all of Mamacita's.

Lee stood easy, his hands at his side, and waited for the sergeant's hand to stop moving along his belt. If it continued to move, Lee would draw and shoot the man, try for the trooper with the second, then back to the sergeant for a finisher . . . then back to the trooper for his. It was, once the fear of death or injury was out of it, much like juggling some noisy, barking indian club in a gentlemen's gymnasium. It was a hand-skill, quick and alternate shooting, only a hand-skill.

The consequences, of course, could be grave—certainly would be, here. With these two dead, providing Lee achieved his four shots very quickly and accurately, the squad-rooms of the *Rurales* and the police would empty like wasps' nests, and those hard-bitten men come to kill him. Even Don Luis would not be able (and would likely not try) to help him out of this. Lee had already killed his allotment of Mexican mounted police.

It would be a long ride out of Sonora. And a long ride thereafter.

The sergeant's hand still moved . . . seconds, and few of those, had passed since Lee answered him. It moved—Lee noticing the sergeant's nails were clean—and then it ceased to move. The hand rested quiet, still two inches from that converted cap-and-ball.

"I will," Lee said, "take your shame-faced silence for all the apology of which a sad animal such as yourself is capable and will be certain to convey my regrets to your captain, that he, a Mexican officer, should be burdened with such an inferior."

The thick brown hand slowly clenched but moved no further along the sergeant's belt.

"Go along," Lee said, "if you can remember where you came from, and I will follow."

"A pregnant pause," play-actors called it.

Then the sergeant shrugged, turned, and marched out. The trooper, however, did not. This fellow indicated that Lee should precede him. A slight and gentle inclination of the carbine's barrel.

Lee, feeling he had pushed his luck quite far enough and weary from a long ride and a hard fight, went before, docile as a Saltillo sheep.

Outside in the street, ill lit by a few smoky pitch-pine flares, the sergeant stolidly marched away, the trooper as dutifully marched behind, and Lee strolled along between them, keeping a casual eye on the sergeant as they walked and looking out as well for horse turds, dog turds, and human turds, too, come to that. Lee still noticed after a moment or two that the sergeant's broad shoulders were shaking.

Lee assumed the fellow was not in tears.

Which meant that the sergeant was laughing.

Nothing proves a man a fool more thoroughly than mistaking another man for one.

"My apologies, sergeant. I enjoy my Spanish, poor though it is, perhaps more than I ought."

The stocky man turned as he walked; his face was red with suppressed laughter. "To hear a *gringo* . . ." he said in his strong Indian accent . . . "to hear a gringo such as you trying to talk like a *caballero!*" This was too much for the sergeant, and he chuckled with pleasure, shaking his head at such a marvel, such an absurdity. "I assure you," he said to Lee, walking backward as he talked—and quite lightly on his feet, Lee noticed—"I assure you that you were funnier than the Don himself!" More chuckles. A considerable demonstration for a man with so much Indian blood.

For an instant, Lee thought the sergeant meant Don Luis de Spania. Then, with a painful jolt of embarrassment, realized that this unprepossessing policeman was referring to Don Quixote. It was a book Lee had tried to read in Spanish and had read enough of to realize this copper had pegged him to a "T." *The man who imagined him-self more than he was.* In this case, a border ruffian with pretensions.

This sergeant, if a brute, was a brute who read. Another reminder not to under-estimate these people. Not to over-estimate Lee McCann, either. It might be, for example, that this sergeant and his trooper had had orders . . . orders not to use violence unless it was necessary. Possibly, otherwise—maybe more than possible— that the sergeant and his man might have made a try, and to hell with Lee's fast gun.

Live a little, learn a little.

Two lessons learned today, or learned again. First—when carrying silver, don't ride into canyon passages, no matter how much they cut the journey. And second, never sell a stranger short.

Two lessons . . . and now, a talk with the Captain.

The Captain was a larger man than the sergeant had been—perhaps a bank robber in his salad days, before he'd taken the government's wage, the light blue coat and silver facings. A big, lazy looking man with small black eyes and a considerable nose. His hands were big as garden spades, and not well cared-for, nails bitten to the quick.

A big man, and sensitive, and looked to be very powerful physically. He wore no weapons, and sat behind his small splintered-top desk, at the back of his small whitewashed office, like a brown bear packed comfortably into its den. He was losing hair at the top of his head and where that was occurring, the local barber (no doubt a sissy Lee knew, named Mercurio Sanchez) had carefully trimmed and oiled and plastered each long black hair across the Captain's head.

Lee had been walked past the *Rurale* squadron's guard-room to reach the Captain's office, and had no notion that the Captain needed to be wearing weapons in his lair. An even dozen very rough cobs had been lounging along the corridor as Lee was shepherded past that guard-room and into Captain Gonsalves' small den.

"Sit," said the bear, and indicated a busted-bottom chair. Lee sat and was glad to do it. His bones hurt. Odd how a fight could bruise a man, and those not even smart or ache till long past the fight being done.

"There has, I understand, been some difficulty," the Captain said and didn't appear likely to say any more. Lee'd learned his lesson; there'd be no showing off his fancy Spanish grammar with this man. He answered the Captain in plain straightforward.

"I was sent here on a mission of business by Don Luis. Four men attempted to rob me at Canyon Rojo. I killed them."

The Captain swallowed that with no sign of indigestion. Thought about it for a moment.

"The horse you brought to this city . . ." (it seemed to Lee that "city" was stretching it for Paso Robles) "the horse you brought to this city is not your horse, then?"

A year before, and a stranger to Mexico, Lee would have thought that an irrelevent question, considering that four men had been shot to death attempting an armed robbery. But that was a year ago. Now he knew better.

"No, sir, it is not my horse. Since my horse was killed in the fighting, I used the animal, which belonged to one of the deceased bandits, to transport the Don's . . . business, and to bring me here to report the attempted robbery."

"You go to cantinas to report attempted robberies?"

"I was foolish not to go to the authorities at once. I also felt the need for a drink."

The Captain, apparently not satisfied with that, sat looking at Lee exactly as a bear might have . . . considering him. Considering the influence of Don Luis, also, Lee supposed . . . the usefulness of four dead bandits to an overworked squadron of police with a hundred thousand square miles to partrol . . . the annoyance of it being a Yankee hoodlum who had killed these four bandits . . . the discomfort of an armed and arrogant *pistolero,* and a gringo at that, who thought nothing of riding into Paso Robles on an animal in no wise his own, whatever his excuse.

The Captain, Lee supposed, was considering all these matters as well as the tried and true police tactic north and south, of beating and jailing anyone seriously brought to their attention. An object lesson —always useful.

Lee, a fighting cock only a few minutes before, was now reluctantly ready to be beaten (if only moderately) and was more than ready to be jailed if that meant a decent night's sleep on a corn shuck mattress, or a wooden bench. He was suddenly tired right down to his toes.

This indifference perhaps made some slight impression on Captain Gonsalves, who, after a minute or two, grunted, told Lee to go and get the horse he did not own, bring it to the military corral, and then to get out of the Captain's sight and to stay out of the Captain's sight.

Lee was happy to do that.

Lee slept.

He slept a long, long, sweet sleep, drugged only slightly by a pipe of marijuana hemp and two or three glasses of mescal.

He slept out the rest of the night and slept through the morning as well—all the

going and coming, the to'ing and fro'ing,
the clatter and chatter, singing and what-
not that saloons and whore-houses produce
in midmorning, with the sun well up and
bean pot put to boil. The women made
enough noise for a wedding, but they never
woke him. Two girls even came into the
room to sweep it out, saw him on the bed,
giggled and retreated. He didn't wake for
that, either.

It was the smell of food that finally
roused him—pinto beans, and chilies, and
roast pork. That, and the coffee. Those
odors woke him and woke him nicely,
slowly, his dreams accommodating to those
rich smells of food, so that he was sitting in
a fine restaurant in the Palmer House in
Chicago. He had ordered a huge dinner and
was smelling it being cooked . . . was somehow also in the kitchens, watching the
beans being cooked, the women sitting in a
row along the black Garland stoves,
patting tortillas while the *Maitre de* tried to
hurry them. The Chicago wind, icy off the
lake, whined past the kitchen windows . . .

He woke, reached for the Bisley Colt's,
and felt the curved butt snug in his hand
(the holstered revolver hanging from the
bed-post) before he was certain where he
was. He had taken to touching the weapon
in that way whenever he woke. A nervous
habit, Lee thought, and unpleasant.

He sat up in the bed, the worn springs

sighing musically, and noticed he was naked. Had not slept in his boots, then. Some sort of civilized going to bed.

Lee recalled his interview with Captain Gonsalves. It might be just as well to get about his business and get out of Paso Robles. He had never known just how far Don Luis' influence, his political power with the revolutionary government, stretched. Likely that waxed and waned depending on which general was appointed where, which governor was in well with Mexico City, which not.

These were matters that Mexicans knew in their bones. And Lee did not.

The *Rurale* Captain—who must be very efficient or very well connected to be posted in Paso Robles rather than some God-forsaken little hole in the desert—might have to take Don Luis' wishes seriously to account. Also, he might not. In fact, he might have some obscure reason to please some obscure person by having Don Luis' gringo pistolero taken out to a corral and whipped, or out to a wall and shot.

Might be waiting for instruction on just such an action.

And Lee had killed two blue-jackets already.

All in all, time to buy another horse (being very careful about the bill of sale), time to get Don Luis' silver out from behind

Mamacita's bar (where it was probably safer) and to the Banco National. And then, time to get the hell out of Paso Robles.

Chapter 5

But now he was hungry as a lobo wolf in midwinter.

He swung his feet to the floor and was just standing when he heard the room door swing open behind him. It was a hard, quick stretch to reach back for the Colt's, to turn to the door with the piece cocked and coming up.

The girl stood pop-eyed—assuming, Lee supposed, that she was about to be shot to rags. A new maid, Lee saw, and raw as could be. A small, stocky country girl. Not too much breast on her, a big head, strong-boned face, brown-black eyes and midnight hair, coarse as a horse's and chopped short. Perhaps fifteen years old . . . more likely a year or two younger.

She had a rough straw broom, was clutch-

ing the handle as it might save her from
gunfire. Had dropped a wad of rags when
Lee'd turned to her.

Lee stepped back to the bed to slide the
Colt's into its holster. "Don't be frightened.
I don't make a habit of shooting girls."

The girl said nothing. Lee saw her glance
flick to his groin, then away. Likely a virgin
bought by Luz or her silent partner from
some *campeseno* family poor as dirt.
They'd have promised the father not to
whore the girl, but would nonetheless, soon
enough.

"Go on, do your work," Lee said, speaking slow Spanish to her, and turned to pick
his clothes off a chair-back beside the bed.
Some of these people spoke no Spanish at
all . . . talked one of any dozen of Indian
dialects instead.

He put on his shirt, then stepped into his
long john pants, turned again to find his
socks and boots, and saw the girl glance
over at him over her shoulder, then recom-
mence dusting down a walnut wardrobe
with enough carving on it to be in the
Viceroy's bedroom, as the local saying had
it for any fancy-work.

Perhaps it was that glance, perhaps the
bowed bare nape, brown as sugar, that
showed beneath the weight of her hair as
she bent her head to her work, perhaps only
the blind hornyness of morning.

Lee, still barefooted, walked round the

bed to her. She stood still as he came close —probably too scared or shy to look around again.

He walked up close enough to touch her ... stood looking down at that dense black hair—clean enough; Luz or her girls must have scrubbed this one with carbolic soap when she came into the place. The girl smelled of that strong soap ... smelled some of sweat, too, and wood smoke from the kitchen fire. She was a small girl—came barely to his chest. Barefoot, her brown feet square-toed and sturdy. Probably never had a pair of shoes. Likely only red-painted *hurashes* to wear to mass. Carry them to the church, put them on, then carry them again on the walk home.

No breasts to speak of—the Indian blood —but looked to have a solid ass on her.

The girl stood quiet before him, frightened even to turn round and look at this strange gringo *pistolero*. There was a sweet smell to her, too. Smelled of girl, was the truth of the matter. That odd, sweet smell that most women had. You could catch it on the street sometimes. Just walking past one or two women walking the other way, you could smell that faint odor. Nothing of made-and-sold perfume about it, either.

This peasant girl had never got within a country smile of store-bought perfume.

Lee saw her small, strong brown hand clutching the broom handle—she'd been doing her dusting left-handed, appeared to think the broom some protection against this strange man—had likely seen her mama dust some drunk drifter off with one, send strange dogs flying out of their mean yard.

The girl's hand was trembling.

Lee heard the voices of other women downstairs . . . heard Pablo Cienfuegos joking with them. Pablo was Luz's bully—a big, fat, strong fellow, as likely to jape a man out of pulling a knife as to crack the fellow's head to prevent it.

"Don't be afraid of me," Lee said. He put his hand on the back of the girl's neck.

It was like touching a frightened horse or laying a hand on the side of the locomotive engine at a railroad station. Same subtle, continuous trembling.

The skin at her nape was smooth as pressed cotton. He slowly slid his fingers up into her hair and she started and made a sound in her throat.

Lee squeezed gently at the back of her neck, not near hard enough to hurt her. Then he spread his fingers down across her cheek and gently pressed there, to turn her head toward him.

She looked up at him from under a coal black fall of hair. Wide eyes full of fear. Her wide mouth fallen half open, lower lip trembling.

Small teeth were even . . . white enough. . .

"I said I wasn't going to hurt you. Now come here." He guided her as much as forced her, keeping his grip on her nape, squeezing gently if she seemed to hold back, drawing her along with him step by step back to the bed.

She was dragging the broom with her, betrayed of any help it might have been. Whatever—it was only straw and stick, now.

Lee reached out with his other hand and gently pulled it from her grip. She clung, and then let it go. She bowed her dark-haired head under his grip as if he were exerting all his power, as if he were crushing her there, squeezing all the strength from her. As if this firm hold was the most dreadful of all grips.

"Come here, now—you do what I tell you. I won't hurt you. You're a decent girl. I would never hurt you . . ."

He drew her to the bed and made her sit down there beside him. She resisted sitting down, and Lee did grip her harder. Then she sat down beside him in a rustle of black cotton cloth, the cloth of her white apron.

"What is your name?" Lee said. "Is it as pretty as you are?" He stroked her neck gently, stroking her lightly under her ears, over the smooth skin just sheltered by her hair.

The girl was weeping, but silently, a few, slow, gleaming tears coursing delicate down the strong planes of her face, shining wet on her cheekbones. One tear had reached her mouth; it glittered in the sunlight, trembling at her upper lip.

Her eyes were tight shut as if what she could not see, would not happen to her.

She began to gasp for breath, at first quietly, then louder. Lee judged she was working up crying out.

He put his hand on the back of her neck again, forced her head down so she sat beside him bowed over. "Don't be noisy, now," he said. "There's no need for it."

Gone wrong here, no doubt of that. Doing a wrong piece of work, no doubt of it at all. A cruel piece of work . . .

His cock was standing up in his underwear, hard enough to hurt him.

Tears were dropping on her little white apron. Some fancy of Luz's—to have her maids decked out like French girls in service. Duds had probably cost more than buying the girl to wear them.

"You cut that out, now," he said, and shook her a little, from side to side. She was pliant as a reed, felt close to fainting. "You dry those tears and cut that crying out."

Obedient as a nigger in Mississippi, the Indian girl picked up a corner of her apron in a shaking hand and daubed at her face with it. When she was finished, she sat still beside him, head bowed beneath his hand.

"Look at this, now," Lee said, and unbuttoned the flies of his underpants so that his cock was out. "Look at that, now." He turned her head with his hand, so that she was looking at it. She was panting softly, like a caught rabbit.

Lee reached over, took one of her hands from her lap, and put it on him. The palm of her hand was wet with sweat. Her hand was shaking as she gripped him. She was looking up at the room door now as if someone—her father, her mother, perhaps, might come by magic from their distant village, might see what she was being required to do . . . might storm into the room by magic or the priest's prayers, with *machetes* and rocks, to destroy this strange and terrible man and save her.

Lee held her by the back of her neck very hard now—he thought he might be hurting her—he pulled the girl half over against him. Then he shoved her head down hard.

She strained back, trying to sit up, her eyes rolling like a terrified animal's. She was a strong little girl. Lee did have to hurt her then; he gripped her so hard that her mouth opened with the pain of it. He put his other hand in her thick black hair, and so forced her head down until her face was pressed awkwardly against his cock . . . her clenching hand.

"You put that in your mouth, now. You do that, or by Jesus Christ . . . !" Truth was, he didn't know what he'd do, except have her do as he wished by any way at all. But the words did his business for him.

Terrified, shaking under his weighting arm, the girl clumsily kissed at the purple, swollen head of the thing she held, then tried to sit up again, to twist free of Lee's grip, as if that single unspeakable thing she had done were more than enough.

But Lee wouldn't let her up.

He pressed her head down again—guiding her, gripping the nape of her neck hard enough to make her gasp with pain. That small desperate Indian face, boned for dignity, was forced slowly down, trembling in resistance, until her soft cheek, then her mouth were held against it.

The girl made a sound, and kissed at Lee's cock again, and he held her to it, managed and maneuvered her head to keep her mouth there and raised his hips to thrust his cock up against her lips, her mouth.

The girl moaned as he gripped her neck still harder and her mouth slowly opened, and his cock slid into her. Lee felt the last resistance, then the rough edges of her parting teeth. Then wet, and heat, and softness . . . the struggle of her tongue as his meat drove up into her mouth.

She moaned and gagged, her throat convulsing. The swollen head of his cock was in her and a few inches more than that. The girl's cheeks were bloated with him.

She gagged again—tried once more to wrench away, to sit up from what she was doing, but Lee wouldn't let her go. He did not, then, care if he killed her.

He shoved her head down hard, seeing her mouth stretched so wide it seemed her jaw must break from it. He held her there, held her head still, his fingers clamped at the back of her neck. Lee's heart was thumping; he was wonderfully excited . . . oddest damn thing, in this small, sunny room . . . like a dream lasting past sleep.

The girl kept her eyes closed, as if what she couldn't see couldn't be happening. She was snorting softly, breathing through her nose, trying not to gag at the size and length of him thrust up into her mouth. Lee could feel the back of her throat at the tip of his cock, feel it gently convulse from time to time against him as the girl tried to keep from retching.

Lee slowly took his hand from the back of her neck, slid his fingers up into her thick, soft hair. Stroked her hair gently for a moment. She didn't try to raise her head from him. Sat quietly, head bent to his lap, the thick, pale, purple-veined cock forcing her jaw wide, thinning her lips as they strained around it.

The girl's brown-skinned throat moved as she gulped to keep from vomiting. Spittle was running in glistening strands from her mouth, running down the length of him, small drops of it clustered in the hair there.

The girl still kept her eyes tight closed.

Lee gathered a handful of her hair . . . slowly lifted her head, just a little . . . then slowly pushed it down again.

Her mouth made a wet noise on his cock as he did that.

He did it again. Lifted her head a little, then slowly thrust her down on the stake of his cock again. The girl snorted, breathing noisily through her nose.

Up—then slowly down again.

Lee felt something seem to soften in her mouth, to stretch deeper.

He let her rest for a moment. Sat feeling almost like a fool for his roughness, his frowardness. Sitting here in a down whoreshouse with his dingus up a maid's mouth. He looked down at the girl's shining black hair, at his fingers tangled in it. Tugged gently . . . felt the hot wet moving slowly up him—the cool of the room air where her mouth was leaving him soaked with her saliva. Felt the slightest touch of her teeth there . . . Then pushed her head down again, a little faster this time.

The girl gulped and gagged—tried feebly to resist him—and Lee pushed down harder. Shoved her head down on him till she heaved and bucked under his hands, retching, strangling on it.

Damndest wish to jam it up all the way. Up into her throat.

Hard to see why she should live, when the four yesterday had died shot to rags ... Not much to death, when you looked at it close. Just like breaking wet clocks, was what it was, and waiting for someone to break yours.

Hard to see why he shouldn't choke this greaser bitch with it.

He had both his hands on her—used one to brush the hair away from her face ... hair as black and coarse as a Chinese girl's. Riles had said the Indians came from China or thereabouts. Hair was surely the same sort ...

He brushed the girl's hair back, ducked his own head to look at her. Damned if women didn't look odd with cocks in their mouths. Odd expressions on their faces ... The girl's eyes were open now, wide, expressionless. Truth was, the poor thing looked dead already. He felt her tongue moving against him. Not so dead then ...

Lee slowly began to move her head again, raising it ... letting it fall. The girl seemed to have given something up—perhaps had given everything up. Her mouth was slack as an old whore's privates. She slobbered on him as Lee moved her head up and down to his pleasure. Made a wet, pumping, sucking noise. Damned it she wasn't near to taking it all.

He took his hands from her hair. For a few moments, like a steam machine slowly running down, the girl continued to suck at him . . . lifting her head, then letting it fall, her mouth as soft and accommodating as if he'd smashed her jaw. She did that for a little while . . . then slowed . . . then stopped, her head poised above him, the fine double tendons on her nape prominent with strain. She still held the head of his cock in her mouth. Held it there in warmth and wet . . . moved her tongue slightly against it. For whatever reason (fear, or some odd surrendering fondness) she suckled it softly.

"That's a honey . . ." Lee said to her in Spanish. "That's my honey . . ." Crooned to her like a lover as she crouched over, the gleaming black helmet of hair almost concealing what she was doing.

Lee reached down and pulled her head back and off him. She left his soaked cock with a damp kissing sound. The thinnest bright thread of saliva ran from her lower lip to the tip of it for an instant, then broke and vanished.

The girl sat supported by Lee's arm, leaning against him as if she were injured or sick. Her soft mouth hung slack as if it could never close. Her chin ran with spit. She looked at him as he'd seen men look that he had shot. Reproachful . . . mildly surprised that such a thing could have happened to them . . . happened to her.

"I was too rough," Lee said. "Wasn't I too rough for such a sweet girl?" He eased her gently back and down, and she lay back obediently across the bed, legs hanging down, small bare brown feet just clear of the floor.

Someone was walking down the hall, a woman by her light step. Down the hall and past the room door. Down to the far end of the corridor. And called out: *"Florenca!"*

Called the name once, then came back down the hall, and on down the stairs. Lee heard music from down there. Someone playing *La Paloma*. Not playing well . . . Playing the song badly on the guitar.

"There," he said to the girl, who was lying staring straight up into the ceiling . . . who did not turn her eyes to look at him, even when he leaned down to kiss her on her bruised, wet mouth. "There," Lee said. "Is that your name—Florenca? It's a very lovely name. It suits you . . ." And kissed her again, gently enough, he hoped, to heal some small part of her hurt.

Chapter 6

Suddenly—and to Lee's great surprise—
the girl turned as she lay, and struck at him
with one small fist. It was an awkward blow
that barely touched him, but it startled him
some.

He gripped her wrists and held her still,
feeling a brute and a fool in equal measure.
"Now, now . . . dammit!" he said, and she
hissed and spat up at him like a kitten.

"Be still, now!" Lee said, "and cut that
out!"

The girl lay panting. Her long black
dress, her apron had flounced up as she'd
struggled. Her brown calves and knees
were bare. Her calves, though round and
smooth, were sturdy as a boy's from
climbing the hills in the back country. Her
knees were scarred from the scrubbing

work she did, kneeling on brick and board and tile.

Having rested for a breath or two, staring up at him, her eyes round and black as California olives, the girl suddenly tried to draw one of his prisoning hands close enough to her mouth to bite it. Lee wrenched his hand away, and stretching her wrists out wide, pinned her to the crumpled bed sheets, bearing down with his weight to hold her there.

His naked cock, still wet from her mouth, still stiff as a wooden billet, rubbed for an instant against the stuff of her dress. That small touch alone sent a jolt of pleasure through him.

"You dumb little bitch," he said to her in English, "you wouldn't know beans if the bag was open!"

Leaned down like the damndest of idiots, and kissed her.

And got the fiercest bite for doing it. The girl caught his lower lip in those small white teeth and bit it almost through.

It hurt like fury but Lee didn't try to pull away. Didn't try to strike her, to force her mouth apart. He just kept on kissing—and tasted blood. He murmured something to her—didn't know what it was, himself. Damn fool . . . Felt like she was chewing that lip right off him . . .

Lay half on her, but as lightly as he could,

kissing . . . kissing her. Felt blood running down his chin. Whispering to her . . . to this ignorant peasant girl. Damn ignorant Indian. Telling her all sorts of things—as well as a man could tell with his lip near riven in two. Stroking her hair . . . must have hurt her, tugging at her hair like that. He stroked it as lightly as he could.

Suddenly felt her sharp teeth ease up. Hurt near as much when she let go as when she'd bit. He was kissing her in a welter of blood. Saying some foolish thing to her about how startled . . . well, how suddenly scared he'd been in Canyon Rojo. Scared shit-loose when those bandit mutts had cut down on him. What that sort of stuff had to do with fucking, damned if he could see. Made him feel better . . . less of a jackass, in some way.

Kissing her . . . tasting blood. Tasting the sweetness of her with the blood.

And she kissed him back.

Soft . . . hesitant, little pecking kisses. More like a child's than a woman's. She put up a hand to touch his face . . . touch his lips where she'd bitten him. She said something, softly.

"Honey . . ." Lee said. "My little honeycomb." He turned half on his side, gathered her up into his arms, and she came to him soft as feathers. "Little honeycomb . . ."

He stroked her hair as if he could caress

away the roughness he had used with her. What a fool, to take anything so pretty, and to hurt it . . .

Her big, dark Indian eyes were open, looking into his own odd amber ones as if she could see straight through him. Faces were close enough for Lee to feel the light touch of her breath on his mouth, the side of his cheek. Her breath smelled of sweet milk and wood smoke.

"Are you a good man or a bad man?" she asked him in Indian-accented Spanish. And waited in his arms, watching his eyes, to hear what he would say. It was a child's question.

"I am sometimes bad and sometimes good. I try not to be too bad a man." Sounded to him like a child's answer, as well, but it appeared to satisfy her. *Florenca.* An unusual name. Something half Spanish, half *Indio*, likely, but it suited well enough.

Startled him as much then as she had by striking at him. She reached down between them and directly took his cock into her hand. She held it for a moment, then commenced to stroke and pet at it, looking all the while into Lee's eyes, and apparently well enough pleased by what she saw there.

Lee was seized by such a pleasure that he felt the jissom rising in him in a terribly sweet pain, and almost let loose of it over her small hand, her stroking fingers. He rose up over her instead, and kissed her hard, driving her head back down into the bedding, and she bucked up against him, her mouth loose and wet under his. The taste of blood was like the taste of a camp knife blade red with the blood gravy of a roast. Lee sucked on the girl's tongue, drew it up out of her mouth to suck and lick at it.

She let him do what he wished.

He kissed her for a long while, finding something new with her mouth somehow through all the kisses. Her slight body seemed to grow under him . . . to become more and more defined the longer he kissed her . . . licking along those small even teeth, touching the slickness and perfection of her inner mouth, her gums, the slippery insides of her cheeks, the neat ridges at the top of her mouth.

He took his time . . . and he learned it all. He gathered in her saliva, and sipped it, little by little. He kissed and worried at her lips, not minding the pain from her bite. Kissed her so hard she gasped for breath, murmured to him to let her breathe.

Then, bit by bit, he forgot all the gentleness that he'd intended and hugged her to him hard—squeezing her, crushing her to him as if he could weld her to him as a smith hammered hot iron to iron.

She groaned, and licked at his throat.

Lee reached down with one hand to gather up the girl's skirts—tugged the cloth up to her thighs—then lifted her to him and pulled her dress and apron to her waist.

She made no move to hinder him.

Lee pulled a little away from her, braced up on his elbow, and looked at her. She lay beside him, wide-eyed, panting like a doe that had been dog-run—her black hair tangled, the plain bosom of her dress rising and falling with her breathing. Below the ruck of black cloth and white apron at her waist, Lee saw she wore little pantelettes of white cotton—looked to be cut from some flour sack, then carefully resewn along the seams. The soft, burnished brown skin of her thighs looked very dark, rich as fine ground coffee against the whiteness of that cloth.

"There, now . . ." Lee said. "There, now . . ." He couldn't take his eyes off that place. Such ordinary stuff, a woman's privates. Not many men who hadn't seen a number of such. Certainly he had seen a passel of such splits . . . shouldn't be in such a sweat, now, about seeing another. Shouldn't be.

He reached down, and gently put his hand on her. Resting it lightly on her thigh. Smooth. Smooth. Glossy smooth. And warm as toast.

She made no move at that, only looked down to watch what he was doing.

Lee slowly slid his hand up to her fork. Slowly . . . slowly, he lifted it . . . then put it gently down on the small mound, still covered in white cotton. It felt like a slight, soft heart, stirring under his palm.

He squeezed at it lightly, and the girl said something in Indian, and put her slender arms up to cover her face.

Lee slid his arm under her waist, lifted a little, and with his other hand, tugged her cotton pantelettes down her thighs to her knees, down her legs and off of her.

Naked. She lay naked for him.

Lee bent over the girl . . . drifted over her, breathed her in. Her naked legs, her groin, the plump little mound of her sex—only sparsely furred—all seemed to glow in the sunlight, gave off a richness of heat and sweet odor (a sharper gluey smell at her crotch) that seemed to Lee finer than a treasure of gold.

He slid down off the bed, crouched at the girl's knees, put his hands on them, and gently pushed them apart. The girl made no resistance to him at all. She lay still, her arms still crossed over her face. Lay as still as if she were asleep. As if she had no notion what was being done to her.

Lee pushed her knees wide, then half rose to lift them higher, push them farther apart. The girl lay still, legs spraddled wide before him. Letting him see everything of her. The slight notch at her cunt had opened a little with the spreading of her legs. Just the slightest moistness . . . barely visible soft rose-pink in a delicate brush of dark fur. Down in the deeper cleft of her buttocks, only the shadow of the small brown button of her ass.

Lee leaned to her, put his hands on the meat of her thighs, and slowly pushed them wider, shoving them farther apart. Looking up, he saw the girl's mouth open under the shadow of her arms. He saw her breathing as he spread her wider to look at her in the bright morning sunlight.

Her thighs strained far apart now in his grip—the great single tendons that ran up into her groin stood out like India-rubber hose. And this had pulled her private place a little wider . . . stretched it almost open. Damp . . . a patch of wetter red. Her asshole showed now, too, the small wrinkled pucker set in a deep crease of darker brown.

Lee crouched before her, and looked, and saw everything that she had ever hidden since she was a naked child.

Then, still gripping her thighs, he leaned forward to taste it.

He leaned forward, and licked very lightly at the jointure of her thigh, the place where the brown skin stretched tight over that great tendon. Her skin was smooth as powdered ice. It tasted of salt sweat, and some deeper, finer taste, like hotel bread, or some sort of cake. He felt a need to bite into it. Would have been pleased enough, if somehow it would not hurt her, to bite into the skin and break it. Bite deeper into the soft, strong meat beneath it. Bite again— deeper still—bite her down to the white bone. Eat into her there until his teeth clicked on bone . . . Leave nothing left of her in the bed, save blood spots . . . wet, chewed hair.

Could carry her away forever, then. He would have her then for good and all. Would have this girl in his belly, to be made into his bones and blood. A man couldn't be so alone who had done that.

If it wasn't a shame to do—if it wouldn't mean hurting . . . killing her. A thought, that was all—a way to get nearer . . . deeper into her.

He licked her spraddled thigh until the skin there was wet and glistened in the sunlight, until all he could taste was his own spit. All he could smell was his own spit.

He turned to her other, to the thigh ridge of that buried tendon, to the tender hollow beneath it. He licked at her there like a dog, nuzzled his face into her, smelling her, lapping at that sweaty, glossy skin, feeling faintly against his cheek the lightest touch of her crotch hair as he moved against her, nipping gently at her skin. Taking just the

littlest bit of her tender skin in his teeth,
hardly closing his teeth on that tenderness
at all. Just the slightest bit.

With his left hand, he raised her right
thigh, lifted it up to make a wonderful
roundness where her buttock became that
thigh in a sweeping thick curve up and up
to the back of the knee. He crouched,
looking at that for a while. He stroked that
weighty curve with his fingers, but couldn't
feel enough; his fingers were too hard, too
calloused, too coarsened by reins and rope,
by whip-butt and horse-tack, by rifle lever
and pistol grip. He couldn't feel enough of
her. Saw now what advantage city men had
over country men and ranchers. Soft
fingers to touch softness with.

He craned his neck and licked at that
curve, licked up the hollows of her knee . . .
tasted soap there, along with a rich taste of
her. All sunny Mexico under his mouth, his
tongue. Then he tried all down the curve,
kissing and gently biting at her. The girl
shifted when he did that. He heard her sigh
and murmur something.

He licked down to the fullness of her buttock and held her knee high while he bent
further, and ran his tongue down the warm,
soft divide of her ass. The girl gasped at
that and tried to shift away, but Lee bent
his head to her again, and kissed her small
rosette, and tongued it. She tried to squirm

away again, but Lee put his hand up onto her neat belly, and held her still.

After a while, he leaned back from her . . . looked at her, her damp buttocks, her slack thighs spread wide . . . brown skin shining with wet from his mouth . . . his tongue. He glanced up at her face. She lay looking back at him . . . an odd kindly look, as if he were some sad fellow standing hungry in the street.

He looked up at the girl. She lay watching his hand, that finger touching her there.

"I won't hurt you," Lee said. He said it in English, but the girl smiled up at him as if she understood.

Lee tried to slip his finger up into her—curled the tip of it up to open her little cunt. Did it with all the gentleness, but even so, felt her wince away. Felt her then stop herself from moving away.

She smiled up at him as if he hadn't hurt her.

A virgin. Of course, a virgin.

Lee crouched to her again, put his thumbs to each side of that small, tender, furred place, and tenderly parted it . . . opened it . . . spread it as wide as he could without hurting her.

Saw into her. A complicated little place. Wet . . . red . . . smelling of the glue of life. Fish glue . . . an ocean smell. Smelled like the shore at San Francisco, all those years ago.

He bent his head and kissed it, then he put his tongue into it . . . pushed it far up into her. Began licking at her, pressing his face against that dampness . . . softness. Feeling the wet against his lips . . . the delicate petals, the slippery pink lacework.

He licked it until the girl groaned and moved restlessly under his mouth. Gasped, and shifted her soft thighs slowly this way and that as he worked on her, biting gently at her now. Kissing, sucking at her.

"Ah . . . Madonna . . ."

Lee stood up from her, then leaned forward, reached down to place the swollen, painful head of his cock against the girl's wet cunt. Then, slowly, he thrust into her.

Thrust in . . . felt the heat and squeezing, the soaked, fur-rimmed hole clenched around him. Thrust slowly . . . slowly further, his arms trembling with the strain as he held himself above her. Then felt . . . something. Something . . . and hesitated.

The girl looked up at him then. Looked up into his face. Looked up with dark eyes that saw everything.

And Lee felt her hands, her arms come up to wrap around him, to bind him to her with soft strong bands. Felt her small hips come suddenly thrusting up against him, up around him in one surge as his cock drove through that maidenhead, broke it, and slid into tight and slippery narrowness.

The girl convulsed under him as he fucked full into her. She took the whole length and size of it, gasping, and he drove it in all his strength.

She was stuck on it, impaled, and she kicked out, drew her legs up high at either side of him, grunting, calling out as he pulled it almost out of her, then slowly shoved it all the way into her again. Lee didn't let her rest. He wanted to let her rest, but he couldn't—and couldn't rest himself. His cock slid nearly out of her with a wet, sucking sound, and he drove it in again. Drove it till they came together with a soft smacking sound, she grunting "Oh . . ." as he struck her.

Lee felt her small strong fingers clawing at his back. When his cock was buried in her, felt her sturdy legs come up to circle his waist, to lock around him so that for an instant he couldn't move, couldn't slide his cock back to thrust into her again.

When she had him locked to her in that fashion, the girl writhed and twisted beneath him, driving herself up deeper onto his cock, biting at his neck as she wrestled with him, sobbing, calling out for her mother.

Lee took her in his hands then and pushed her down, held her hard down on the bed and fucked and fucked into her. Willing enough to kill her with it now. His cock, as it pulled almost out of her, was oily with her juices, streaked with the blood of her torn maidenhood. As he wrestled, riding her, Lee reached with one hand beneath them both, searched for her small asshole, found it, and slowly screwed a sweat-wet finger up into her there.

The girl meowed like a cat when he did that, and tried to clench her buttocks against him, but Lee pushed the finger up into her—felt through some wall of flesh there his cock entering her as well, and heard the girl began to scream—saw her head thrown back, the veins standing from her throat—and felt himself begin to go . . . begin to slide away from this to something else. Something that began to tear itself out of him in great throbbing spurts. It swept him away from his life . . . away from everything.

It was more than enough pleasure to die with.

He lay balanced on the girl as if they were floating on the waves of the sea. He dreamed his pleasure, it was so great, and came and came into her . . . felt closer to her than anyone. Felt much closer to her . . . than to anyone . . .

Chapter 7

Lee woke to late afternoon.

He'd slept as if he hadn't slept the night before, and woke feeling wonderful . . . stretched out on the rumpled, stained sheets until his bones cracked . . . drew great breaths of air, smelled the rich stinks of Mexico from the alley outside, the delicate odors the girl had left behind her.

He hadn't known when the girl had left him.

He stretched again, listening to the noises downstairs. Mamacita's was warming to its work. Then he swung his feet to the floor, stood, and went to the chair to get his duds. He'd dress, go down to the kitchen for breakfast (and it would be a considerable breakfast—beans, fried pork, a stack of tortillas, eggs, coffee). Have his breakfast, then go out to the stable yard for a bath and shave. Get a clean shirt on, then, clean underwear as well. Clean socks.

Then to the bank with Don Luis' silver pesos.

And then?

Out of Paso Robles, for certain, once he'd bought a horse. Go to Choo-choo's for the horse. Man was a thief, of course, but sold good stock. Get a big horse perhaps this time. A big gelding with an even temper if the trader had such. An easy-riding horse, too, if possible. Too damn much jolting and jarring, riding these Mexican tracks.

As to the girl . . . As to her, payment for what he owed. Had used her, and used her rough. Needed to pay for that as much as that could be payed for. Luz would likely make a whore out of her now.

Not Lee's fault—well, his fault in a way. No girl could work in such a place for long and not be turned to the life by someone.

Lee pulled on his boots, took his gunbelt from the bed post, looped it over his shoulder, and walked out of the room and down the corridor to the stairs. Looked like a handsome sunny day and not too hot, though Lee had missed the noon of it.

The kitchen at Mamacita's, like most such down here, was half kitchen and half back porch, open to the yard and alley. More chickens running in the kitchen than the yard. A thin old man named Eusebio cooked for the place—was a devil with chilies and chocolate cooking, almost as good with the rest. Eusebio was at his fat black wood-burner this afternoon, minding his business for dinner. Smelled like rabbit stew (and hot enough to burn in the smelling).

Four women were sitting in a row against the side wall, patting tortillas.

The girl was one of them, second from the right.

She looked up when Lee walked in, looked up and smiled at him as bright as the day.

Lee barely nodded to her, then nodded to Eusebio and walked on through. No use making up to her . . . no use playing true love.

He went down the steps into the yard and heard the other women laughing at her. He went to the pump and dragged the big washtub over.

The women would be having a good laugh at her in there.

That foolish smile of hers . . . A smile looked damned odd on an Indian face, anyway. Up to her, did she decide to make an ass of herself . . .

He pumped in a good half tub-full, the water coming up from a way, and cold. Then he went across the yard and into the stable, looking for soap. Found a sliver, dark yellow and hard as stone, on a shelf with toothless curry-combs and a hide brush with pitiful few bristles left to it.

He went back to the yard, and hung his gunbelt on the pump handle. He started to unbutton his shirt—then stopped and buttoned it up again. Walked back to the kitchen steps and up them, saw the row of women still sitting there against the wall, working. The girl had her head down now as she should have had before.

Lee went over to her, waited till she looked up at him, then made her a proper gentleman's bow, reached down to take one small, flour-whitened hand, and bent to kiss it.

Silence in the kitchen.

No noise of patting tortillas, either.

"*Senorita,*" Lee said to her, "I will be having a late breakfast. Would you be kind enough to join me then? For coffee, if you have already eaten?"

The girl stared up at him, tears still in her eyes from the women's laughter. She was, Lee saw, really a handsome girl—not beautiful, to be sure, but pretty enough for a little *mestizo*.

"Until then," Lee said, and leaned down again to brush a strand of that coal black hair from her eyes.

The bathwater had pumped into the washtub cold as cold could be, and would have made for uncomfortable bathing but for the sun. Lee sat up to his belly in the tub

—might as well have been sitting naked in snow—but felt at the same time the afternoon sun battering down hot as blazes on his head and shoulders, his arms, stinging his unprotected forehead.

It made for a pleasure of contrasts that even the stone-hard soap couldn't spoil. Always a fine feeling to be getting clean in any case, even if it took harsh scrubbing.

He scrubbed and he soaped and paid no heed to the Mexicans. Give them their due, they were a modest people, and wouldn't stand about (as some Ameerican louts and whores well might) peeping as a fellow bathed. He bent his head and scooped up handfuls of the cold water to soak his hair. Had never cared for lice—saw no need to have the damn things. Scrubbed and lathered, scrubbed again, rubbing his fingertips hard through his hair. This damn soap should kill anything . . . Smelled like a tannery, pulp mill, and kerosene works combined.

Lee could see, just past the side arbor, a space of the street in front, and kept an eye on that as he bathed, looking for light blue jackets in case Captain Gonsalves decided some brusque action was appropriate after all.

Would be the devil to pay, though, rushing about this yard stark naked, scattering chickens and shooting at *Rurales*. Unlikely to end well . . .

When he'd finished bathing, Lee whistled for a little boy—called him Charlie, the cook's son (or nephew)—and the boy came running with one of Luz's old sheets, the cotton worn to gauze beneath the haunches of her whores, the materian torn and latticed here and there by the spurs of hasty vaqueros, kicking in their joys.

Lee stood, stepped out gingerly onto hard-pan mud and chicken shit, and toweled well off, some bits of the sheet coming away in his hands at too vigorous rubbing. Finished that and finished fast, the sun doing much of his drying for him. Lee wrapped the frayed sheeting around his waist, bent over his bit of mirror at the pump taking care that the harsh sunlight didn't flash from it into his eyes, shook his razor open, and commenced to scrape his beard away. That completed, and a rub of coarse salt from the kitchen across his teeth with a chewed twig-end, succeeded by a hair combing (and another check for nits) and Lee would be toileted and ready for his late breakfast, a visit to the bank, a stop at the horse-coper's—and a drift out of town.

A woman named Eustacia, wide in the beam as any rowing boat, brought them their breakfast under the trellis arbor. This narrow side porch, dapple shaded from the worst of the sun, was the most pleasant place to eat a meal that Lee had found in

Paso Robles. If Luz had had no girls at all in her establishment, even no bar-room and drinkery, she would still have had Lee's custom for this eating place and its food.

A pot of scalding coffee, oddly cooling in the heat; brown sugar and sweet milk to put into it; syrup rolls, small and sticky; eggs scrambled with chilies and green sweet pepper; a basket of tortillas, piping hot and soft as linen napkins; and a platter of shredded pork *tobasco*. It was—even without the fried chicken skin, the bowl of double-cooked beans—enough of a breakfast for two ordinary hungry men.

Lee cleaned the plates handily all by his lonesome—or nearly, Florenca having only a small cup of the coffee, only one syrup roll to nibble.

Odd, how things—people, and their remembered places—would return to sound in a man's mind as if they were just now fresh minted. Lee, sitting in foliaged sunlight deep in Old Mexico, sitting across from a simple girl he had outraged (no nicer word for it, and plenty uglier) remembered suddenly, as if a person had reached out and struck him, another restaurant . . . a backyard place, but elegant. A real restaurant, some might say, not just a greaser whorehouse with a kitchen, and in that back-yard, a laughing dudish fellow (looked the sissy but was not) in a colorful coat. Ned Bierce in a green velvet coat, smiling, joking . . .

just before, their lunch over, he had made
that sad rough go crawling down the street.

Something about this breakfast—a
"brunch" as Bierce would have called it—
had brought that amusing fellow to mind.
Bierce would, Lee supposed, have had
something cutting to say about would-be
gentlemen who found their level in dining
with maids.

Lee regretted some of his killings—regretted them all, at least for a time (had
nightmares . . . other manifestations of
regret almost every occasion of a killing).
But he had never ceased to regret shooting
Ned Bierce to death. Seemed to him he'd
never been the same man after that.
Seemed that he'd killed a friend, though of
only short acquaintance and though Bierce
gave him no choice about it.

"You don't wish for more of a meal than
that, little one?"

The girl, Florenca, smiled at him and
shook her head. She seemed pleased enough
to sit and watch Lee pig it sturdily through
the half-dozen dishes. Seemed to give her
some satisfaction to watch him eat. Not the
first time Lee had noticed that women
enjoyed watching men (those they were
pleased with) fill their faces with food. Had
something to do with the pleasures of nurs-
ing children, Lee supposed.

As to the girl being pleased with *him*, she
certainly seemed to be. Though Lee was

under no illusion that an Indian girl, having been raped (one of those uglier words) might not smile a considerable while before deciding to try to cut his throat.

Yet there appeared none of that in the air. Whether because he had finally given her pleasure, and a pleasure both great and new to her, or because he had honored her with gentlemanly attention after the other women laughed, or because he was white and a *Norte Americano* (though, of course, Mexicans also, were also *Norte Americanos,* at least by geography)—or simply because he was her first man and had broken into her and forced her close, and had therefore caught some cord to her heart, the girl seemed mighty fond.

Mighty fond.

Of course, he had not ended by forcing her. Had been gentle with her, then.

That might have made some difference to her.

Lee smiled back at the girl, then went to scraping up the last of his eggs. No saying that Eusebio couldn't cook an egg. First trial and test of a stove-man, McCorkle used to say. "They can do a egg simple, or they can't."

There now arose some slight question what he was to do with her. Ordinarily, that wouldn't have arisen—a whore being a whore, and situated where she chose to be. Difficulty here was the girl was no whore, not yet. Difficulty was, she would soon be one, her cherry being busted.

"Tell me, little flower," Lee said, taking the last syrup roll since she refused it. "Tell me—do you wish to stay here? Do you wish the life of the other women here? It is not so unpleasant, you know, though you have to do with rough people, not gentle."

A real choice—and by no means a bad one —for a girl from some desperate peasant family living like pigs in a muddy pueblo in the mountains. For most of these women, whoring was a life of luxury and not work at all, as peasant women counted work. In any case, he had asked, and if she chose to stay and live the life . . . well, it was something he need not concern himself with.

The girl put down her coffee cup (she had been holding it with two hands, like a child) and said, "I would like to go."

Eusebio's eggs suddenly felt a little heavy in Lee's stomach.

"You don't want to stay here?"

"No."

An Indian of few words. Eusebio's eggs had definitely been a little overcooked this afternoon.

"Well—would you prefer to go back to your home?"

"No." An Indian of *very* few words.

"Florenca, tell me where you would like to go."

"I will go where you wish," she said,

picked up her coffee cup again in both hands, and took a small sip.

It was near ruining Lee's brunch.

"You can't ride with me, little one."

Nod. Lee was grateful for it. All that was needed was for him to be dogged by some stupid Indian girl. Trailing him in and out of saloons and so forth . . .

"I will go where you tell me . . . *Senor* Lee." The last, the naming of his name, doing mighty quietly.

"Very well then," Lee said, and stood up from the table feeling he'd had his brunch and then some, "I will consider it."

It would cost him money, for the start. It was wonderful, when a man thought of it, how many matters cost money.

Luz Obregon turned her blind eye on Lee, and apparently a deaf ear as well. Showed him her scrawny, dark profile while she counted off a stack of IOU's into her cash box.

"I'll pay the girl's debt off to you and add a gift for the house."

No reaction to "pay"—some reaction to "gift."

"Five pesos for the girl. Two extra for the house."

Fierce Luz appeared to find a particularly rotten IOU. She stared down at it as if the devil had come to Paso Robles to tuck it into her cash drawer. *"Gomez!"* For a thin woman, Luz had a fearsome voice.

She only had to call once. Gomez, a very handsome young man and overseer of the chuck-a-luck wheel, came hustling down the bar combing his hair and smiling in a propitiatory sort of way. It was he, apparently, who had accepted the IOU.

Mamacita held the offending paper out to handsome young *Senor* Gomez. When he had examined it carefully, grinned, rolled his eyes, and shrugged a "foolish me" shrug, Luz leaned further forward, tapped at the young man's lips with the folded IOU as if knocking on a door, and when the sad fellow reluctantly opened his mouth, tucked the paper in as if into a letter box.

Then the lady stood back to watch Gomez chew and swallow that particular promise to pay.

Lee stood by till Gomez loped off back up the bar through a heat-struck afternoon crowd, his lesson learned.

"Seven pesos for the girl. Five for the house."

At which, the meager woman cast him a one-eyed glance, and said, "You are a bad man." She made a delicate gesture, thrusting her forefinger through two others, circled.

"Seven, and five."

Luz considered, the lid faintly trembling, half closed, over her blind eye.

"Take it or leave it," Lee said in English. It was a phrase which seemed as under-

117

standable to Mexicans as to Americans. No translation needed.

Mamacita appeared to understand it very well. She pursed her narrow lips, ticked her long fingernails on the edge of the cotton-wood bar in a hat-dance rhythm for a measure or two. Then she said, "O.K." and held out her hand.

Chapter 8

The *Banco National,* housed in an impressive building—which it should be, having been a small cathedral before the revolution—had nonetheless, Lee suspected, some shortage of ready funds. The echoing, vaulted space (cut red stone, marble facings, the vault set neatly into the place once held by the high altar) was served by only two clerks, neat young men with flat oiled hair and ink-smudged cuffs, and a bank officer, a large soft-bellied fellow with a face like a fish, and wearing a fine English suit.

The bank guard was barefoot and sleeping by the door, a split-stocked breech-loading carbine by his side. Nothing special for protection there; the real protection was lounging in the *Rurale* barracks the other

side of town. Men who robbed this bank
would have their running cut out for them
. . . a long, long run.

There were only two other customers in
the place—local merchants, it seemed. Lee
supposed that most Mexicans were keeping
their cash money under their house floors,
at least until it was known that Diaz would
be able to stick in Mexico City.

"I will give you a receipt in my own
hand," the bank officer said in reassuring
style, as if Don Luis might lose all track of
his accounts without it.

"That would be very useful, *Senor,*" Lee
said, hefted the saddlebags and slung them
down on the marble counter with a more
than sufficient jingle and thump. "You
might care to count it . . ."

"No, no, no." The bank officer shook
fragrant jowls (Bay Rum and oil of
Gardenia, Lee thought). "Not necessary,
Senor McCann."

Fellow appeared fearful of questioning
the Don's honor, even second-hand. An odd
way of business the Mexicans had. Who
you were was more important, sometimes,
than what you had in cash or property.
Politics always had to be taken into
account, even more than in the States.
Family matters were a good deal more
important than business matters—in that,
not like the States at all.

Did he bring such a sum to an American

bank, there would be receipts signed and
cash counted, and no nonsense about it,
even for a Vanderbilt—in fact, especially for
a Vanderbilt. Well . . . the perfumed bank
officer was at least writing out a receipt,
though taking Lee's word on the amount.
He was writing, Lee could see, with great
swoops and scrolls, dashes and darts of
India ink. Flourishes. It would be a hell of a
receipt.

When Lee left the bank—something relieved, in truth, to be shut of the responsibility for the Don's cash (he had no
illusions that Don Luis would ever forgive a
loss of cash)—he found Paso Robles in slow,
stirring, post-siesta ferment.

In this golden late afternoon light, with
shadows stretching long across the cobbled
pavements, the citizens of the town had re-
appeared, refreshed and ready for
marketing, for strolling, for preliminary
ogling of the few decent women out for a
breath of air, for work where essential, for a
drink perhaps at the *Tres Toros* or *Casa-
blanca*. Some *very* decent women, and these
of the better class, were on their way to
church, ensconced in creaky old equipages,
driven by men as old and rheumatic as their
carriages. These ladies sat wrapped in
layers of black bombazine, black lace, black
stuff of every sort. Even their necklaces
were of jet. Their faces, dead pale, occasionally mustached, were set to the front

(no peeking here or there—certainly no peeking at a Yankee *pistolero* booting down the street toward Choo-choo's corral and horse copery. No peek at such as that. These ladies went to church every day, thrice on Sundays, and would have as happily seen a heretic burned, were such still possible in these degenerate times, as seen a horse thief hung or a friend's daughter disgraced.

Lee thought these proud, stupid ladies quite formidable, and saw that they stood like rocks in this town and all others throughout Mexico, no matter what the bandits or generals or *politicos* or *socialistas* were up to in Mexico City.

He enjoyed them, and liked to watch them ride out to church, occasionally with a petulant but defeated son or daughter in convoy.

He had never seen any Mexican—even drunk, even savage—offer to offend these pale-faced, black-feathered turkey hens.

So he stood to watch them rattle slowly by, and swept off his *sombrero* and made his bow as if he were acquainted. Never, not once, had any of these ladies deigned to notice him. Lee would have been disappointed in them if they had.

Choo-choo kept his stable down by the tracks—had, in fact, won his nickname for his love of railroad trains; used to go down to watch the damn engines come in. Still did, Lee supposed. Hard to see why a man would like railroad trains. Lee hadn't cared for them for many years.

It was a fair walk across town, and Lee enjoyed it, despite the heat. Two or three men nodded to him on the street . . . not many. Others knew him well enough, but didn't nod to him. No women appeared to see him, except one selling oranges.

Two little boys walked after him for a while, strutting and pretending to put their hands on the butts of holstered pistols. Then they walked up alongside him for a stretch, asked him questions . . . asked him how many men he'd killed . . . asked him if he'd ever seen a gasoline machine . . .

A few loafers were hanging in at Choo-choo Morelos'. Town roughs, town philosophers, town tramps. Some boys in love with horses . . .

Choo-choo, a tall, gap-toothed drink of water with a handlebar mustache and skin the color of mud, came out of a holding pen to give Lee a vigorous handshake, a commiserating smile.

"I understand that Captain Gonsalves has left you afoot, Mister McCann. Ah, what troubles the police bring upon us, to take from a man his means of riding . . . to reduce him to a peasant, a foot-stomper."

"Troubles indeed," Lee said. "Though, of course, the good Captain was only doing his duty."

"Certainly," Morelos said. "His duty."

"Trot me out some horse-flesh, Chooey, and don't waste our time with dog food." Under no illusions, of course, that Morelos wouldn't try a stunt or two, regardless.

Choo-choo whistled and a dwarf named Pepito went waddling into the west stable, a long shed with perhaps fifteen stalls. It was this stable, Lee had noticed, that Morelos went to some pains to keep clean. The only one, at least, that had a manure pile in front of it, in preference to a stable floor so paved, as with his shed to the east of the tracks.

The dwarf had hustled and soon enough came flying out of the stable door hanging onto the reins of a slab-sided sorrel with a splint thrown on his left fore.

Lee didn't look further, but waved to the dwarf to lead the animal back inside.

"You're wasting my time."

"You're right," Choo-choo said. "I'm at fault in having such a fool in my employ." He shouted to the dwarf to wake up in there! To be a little less of an ass!

And in a minute or two the dwarf came leading out again, and this a considerable animal. A bay gelding, and big as a house. Good bone. Good conformation. Seemed slightly shy, but that might be from being stall-bound. Mexicans thought exercise was wasted on a horse.

The dwarf held the big bay's head while

Lee checked its teeth . . . its eyes . . . ran his hands down the animal's legs.

This was no stable plug. It looked a formidable horse.

"I regret to tell you," Morelos said, "that this beast is a four-hundred-peso beast."

Lee said nothing to that but took the reins from the dwarf, slung up onto the bay's bare back, and booted him out at a run.

Animal sprang right away and ran like a wolf.

It was a pleasure to be up on him, to feel the great lengths of muscle shift and bunch. Feel the wind of the run come fluttering at your face . . .

Lee galloped the bay out across the flats, listening to the horse's beathing, listening for a lunger's whistle and heave.

Nothing. The animal ran steady as a machine—none of the surge and slacken of an off-center runner. A pleasure to ride and easy on the ass, even bareback.

Lee heard the men shouting to him from the stable, urging the *gringo* to boot the beast up, to make the sluggard fly. He reined to a row of chicken coops behind the Street of the Processions, thundered past a group of children who shouted in excitement at such speed and commotion through a late, hot afternoon, then reined the horse left along a dry wash and down that and out into the flats again, very happy with the animal, and determined to buy it—but not for four-hundred pesos.

It was only with the bay drawn back down to a walk that a notion occurred to Lee—the horse, although high-strung, not having swerved in its run at all when the children had shouted on its right side. The notion occcuring, Lee leaned out to the right and sharply clapped his hands by the bay's right ear.

No notice taken. No notice taken of hand-clapping beside the left ear, either.

Lee drew the Bisley Colt's and fired two fast shots, right and left alongside the horse's head.

No notice taken.

He rode the animal on in, swung down, and handed the dwarf the reins. Didn't have to say anything to Morelos. A deaf horse was, sooner or later, a dangerous horse. Constantly wary of surprise, they sooner or later spooked at the wrong time and broke a man's leg . . . or his neck.

"You're still wasting my time."

Choo-choo Morelos was not a horse-coper for nothing. "You might not have noticed," he said. "Am I to be blamed if a man is ignorant . . . or careless? All honor to you that you were not!" And waved the dwarf back into the stable.

"Now," he said, "no more tricks." He combed his handlebar mustache with his thumb and forefinger. "From now, simply a matter of good judgment."

And out came Pepito, dancing along at the end of the reins of a neat grey—very clean-lined legs, a nice, fine head. Animal was shifting as it trotted—likely stable-bound. Good enough gait to it.

Lee went up carefully, thinking there might be a fault of temper there. But the grey had quiet eyes. Held well to have its mouth, its teeth looked at. A young horse, and lively. It sidled and danced a bit while Lee had hold of the bridle, constantly picking its neat feet up and putting them down. Something like a little boy, held fast in church, and having to pee.

Lively. A handsome horse.

Very lively in the foot.

Lee stooped and picked up the right fore. Nothing appeared to be the matter . . . hoof clean, frog sound enough. Went beside and picked up the hind hoof. Horse stood still very nicely for that; dwarf had no trouble holding the reins.

Nothing wrong to see there, either. Lee bent his head to smell the hoof for rot or pus. Sweet as grass. Nothing there to smell.

He put his thumb to the center of the frog there, pressed gently—and the grey snorted hard and suddenly jerked its hoof free, wrenching Lee's wrist a little. Started away and shied in an uneasy half circle, dragging the dwarf in doing it.

It was unusual to find a sound horse with a case of tenders . . . hoof frogs that bruised at any touch, any punishment on the road. Something a very few horses were born with. It rendered them quite useless for riding, for work of any kind.

Lee had heard of sulphur soaks doing some improvement, or sea-water for a few months. Some horse doctors cut nerves deep in the hooves to stop it. Lee doubted any of those remedies worked well.

Sad horse, so handsome and fine, and must have been traded again and again as its fault was swiftly found out. Some impatient man would sooner or later attempt to beat that fault away. End by shooting the beast that, looking so fine, only made mock of its purchaser.

"I have time for one more horse," Lee said to Morelos. "You might try a sulphur soak on this one's hooves. I've heard that sometimes does."

The roughs and philosophers and tramps meowed a few catcalls at the coper—liking, no doubt, to see the biter bit—but Choochoo kept his poise. "It is," he said, "completely unnatural for a Texan to so well know horses." Most Americans were Texans as far as most Mexicans were concerned—those violent people, cold and hot at once, that lay above the Rio Bravo, having made over the century an indelible impression.

Choo-choo sighed at the roughage of a businessman's lot and waved the dwarf away with the sore-footed horse.

It began to seem that Lee must buy private in the town. Some individual's horse . . . It would take time, certainly the rest of the day. Perhaps into tomorrow.

Shortly, the dwarf came scrambling out of the west stable again, leading a stocky black with a head like a carpenter's hammer. The beast had a no-nonsense trot —lifted its knees decently high—and had black hooves, not too large, and seeming as dense as stone.

Lee had seen its like a thousand times. A stump-puller, a jolt-trotter with a deep chest and haunches wide enough for a two-hundred-pound whore to ride pillion.

He had a fated feeling, a vision of himself on just this unromantic and ugly engine. A goer for sure, harsh as a hoof rasp and as tough. Not all that young, either.

A horse. A distillation of horse.

He walked up to check the creature anyway. It stood, lower than his shoulder, silent, still, gazing off into the last haze of afternoon light.

Damn thing looked roughly carved of coal.

Lee looked at its teeth. Not all that young

a horse.

Checked its hooves. Just as hard as they looked.

It was an inescapeable horse.

Lee glanced at Choo-choo Morelos. And Choo-choo knew.

"I will pay you one hundred and fifty pesos for this horse. Take it or leave it."

Choo-choo smiled, as pleased as if the *El Presidente* was pulling into the Paso Robles station, whistle blowing, for his delectation alone.

Chapter 9

Lee rode his new horse back to Mamacita's at a hard jog trot. The black would gallop, and fast enough, but evidently considered that gait to be unnecessary, for he slowed from it whenever Lee stopped batting at him with the crop. The jog-trot, however (and a bone-breaker) the black appeared to regard as a horse's most natural and becoming stride, and, to be fair, he gave evidence of being able to keep that pace up for several days, if watered at intervals, like one of Choo-choo's railroad trains.

Lee decided to call the animal "Horse."

And rode this blocky, unlovely, mechanical beast into Mamacita's side alley alongside the trellised arbor to discover he had visitors, unexpected company, sitting at the arbor's back, sipping coffee in a soft, early evening shadow.

Two of them.

One, a vaquero—a gun-handy fellow named Miguel Onofrio, a soft-looking man, continually sighing when one stood near him, who wore two double-action parrot-gripped .38's in fancy Buscadero holsters on his hips. Onofrio was supposed to have done some ten or eleven men to death, and Lee supposed that could be so. Fellow had damp, earth-colored eyes; didn't appear moved by much, one way or another.

The second visitor, looking mighty high and aloof and looking mighty disdainful of Onofrio as a coffee-sipping partner, come to that, was Don Jaime Alvarez—no "Don" at all, actually, but certainly just as good as most real such, since he was *domo major,* or grand steward and domestic of Las Sabrinas—and appearing much more the hidalgo than the real Don Luis.

They'd come to see him, no doubt about it. Onofrio's thick gaze had been glued to him since the black came thudding down the alleyway.

Don Jaime didn't trouble to look up. He had very elevated airs. Was dressed as fine as a silver dollar, too—black charro suit, braided gold along his lapels, at his cuffs, a sombrero of fine hammered felt (black as night but for its trim of gold braid). Don Jaime looked the grand *haciendado* to the life—these fine clothes, a high-bridged nose as proud as Satan, tiny needle-pointed goatee, grey eyes as frigid as a Castille winter.

Hard to believe the fellow was simply a puffed-up servant, a housekeeper on the grand scale, Don Luis' butler-in-chief and overseer of the household. Not that these were unimportant roles. They were not. Even as Don Luis' shadow, the fellow swung more weight than most in Sonora . . . would have no trouble getting an interview with the Governor himself, come to that.

Not an inconsiderable fellow, for all his charro airs. And, of course, there was Miguel Onofrio. Also, in his way, a considerable fellow.

Lee booted the black over to the raised porch and found himself, with some embarrassment, lifting his sombrero to "Don" Jaime. Mexican ways were catching and the fellow's fine airs had some effect after all.

As he made the courtesy, Lee noticed the girl, Florenca, standing at the kitchen door, watching him. Young fool probably thought he was a dandy dasher, greeting such a lordly acquaintance.

"Good afternoon, Don Jaime," Lee said, making no sport of the title.

"Evening, surely," Don Jaime said, looking out over his coffee cup at the shadows stretching across the yard. "We see you well, I suppose, *Senor?*

"Very well, thank you."

Onofrio had nothing to say. He sat facing Lee, his plump hands relaxed in his lap. Lee got that picture of the fellow in his mind and held it there. Any sudden change in the fellow's way of sitting . . . any sudden movement of his hand . . .

For a few moments, Don Jaime had nothing else to say. He and Onofrio sat like frogs at the edge of a pond, Don Jaime sipping, Onofrio doing nothing at all.

After this pause, Don Jaime put down his cup with a tiny click of china against china. Luz had served this grandee on her own dishes.

"Would it please you to join us, *Senor* McCann?"

"A pleasure indeed," Lee said, and keeping Onofrio in mind, swung down from the black's bare back, went to the porch steps, walked along the planking to them, and took the chair Don Jaime indicated across the table.

Onofrio, Lee found, had a not unpleasant odor of manure about him—odd, since as far as Lee knew, the man pushed no stock at all.

"The Don," Don Jaime said—and there was no doubt as to whom he referred—"is most pleased with your actions in Canyon Rojo."

Pesos saved, bandits dead. And the Don

demonstrating how much he knew, and, thanks to the telegraph, how soon.

Lee said nothing to that, maintained a modest silence. He'd noticed some time ago that people preferred fighting men to remain as silent as possible, assuming, he supposed, that that betokened determination. People who assumed that, he thought, had never met Harvey Logan.

Miguel Onofrio, now—here was a classic of the silent sort of *pistolero*. Fellow sat still as stone, smelling of manure, his hands quiet in his lap.

"I am now," Don Jaime said, "*en route* to La Sabrinas, on a mission of some importance."

French linen bed sheets; Mason jars for the pantries; sacks of Kentucky grass seed; a payroll of several thousand pesos; denim material by the hundreds of yards; German serving platters; Saltillo *serapes;* Colt's Best Revolving Firearms by the case; ammunitions innumerable; liquors and wines by the tun; a purchase (forced or voluntary) of an additional grazing space of some 50,000 hecteres . . . it was matters such as these that constituted Don Jaime's domain, and all in service to Las Sabrinas and its lord.

"All the more the honor you do me in making this visit," Lee said, "in interruption of more important matters."

Don Jaime considered this, found it a

reasonable attitude, and nodded pleasantly. It was always a surprise to discover a *gringo* with any delicacy, any courtesy at all.

"And yet," the Don said, "there is some slight affair that might be usefully brought to your attention, I suppose . . ." He picked up his coffee again, sipped at it, and finding it cool, made an unpleasant face. "Some slight affair . . ." he said, setting the cup down again. "The manager . . . the 'engineer' at Los Gatos has purchased a ticket on the express to Tampico, intending, we presume, to mount that express tomorrow night at the station in Hermosillo or at a nearer stop."

"A long trip," Lee said.

"Yes—but not as long as the next, for this 'engineer' has also purchased by Federal mail a steam-ship ticket from Tampico to Buenos Aires."

"A very long trip, then," Lee said. "Extremely long. I hadn't known it was his time of leave from the mine."

"It is not," said Don Jaime, "his time of leave from the mine."

Lee was not foolish enough to wonder how this Don and the other far more important Don had discovered Max Thornhill's travel plans. He could wonder how Thornhill, a tall, disagreeable German-Scot, born in Mexico but considering himself in no way part of it, could have been stupid enough to assume that the manager of one of the richest small silver mines in Sonora would not be under observation by the owner of that silver mine.

The man was worse than an ass.

Likely, he was dead.

"A robbery of some kind?"

"So we assume," said Don Jaime, staring down into his coffee cup as if the stuff might turn hot again.

Lee glanced over to the kitchen entrance, saw the girl, Florenca, watching him, and lifted his hand as if he had a cup in it, then indicated the Don.

The girl popped out of sight.

"*Senor* Thornhill has become too ill to travel?"

"He has not," the Don said. "He is still in perfect health, as far as I know. Has made new friends, also, it appears."

The Don seemed after a few moments to have nothing more to add and was only roused when Florenca, approaching the table with a good deal of hesitation and one awkward curtsey, placed a fresh cup and a small flowered China coffee pot before him. The Don nodded to acknowledge the service, said, "Clumsy thing," of Florenca, and poured and commenced to sip at his coffee.

"That she is," Lee said, "though, I believe, an honest girl. I doubt if even you, Sir, could train her up to Las Sabrinas standards.''

The Don, like many foolish-seeming men, was no fool at all.

"Is that some whore of yours, *Senor,* that you think to foist on the service of Don Luis?''

Miguel Onofrio stirred ever so slightly in his chair. His plump hands hadn't moved. His shoulders had moved a little.

Lee, pinked once, decided against fencing with a fencer.

"I have been with her once. She was a virgin, a girl sold from the hills into this place. She is a good girl, nonetheless, and a Christian. She wishes to leave this place for some other place both decent and peaceful.''

Having said that much, Lee shut up.

The Don stared down his long nose at Lee, as if in renewed astonishment at the ways of the savages of the north.

"What a romantic tale,'' he said, "and too nonsensical not to be true.'' Another sip of coffee. "We will take her with us when we go. She can ride on top of the diligence with the baggage. She will learn our ways at Las Sabrinas . . . in the linen room, I think, to begin . . . or she will prove herself a fool, or lazy, and so be given to the vaqueros for their amusement.''

Lee had no notion the Don would forget

this favor owed nor fail to request repayment in his own good time.

"An act of Christian charity, Don Jaime."

"What, in the name of Our Lady," said Don Jaime, "can a Protestant know of that?" and so closed the subject.

Onofrio spoke up then, his voice as slow and sleepy as he seemed. "This Thornhill met three *Tejanos* in the pueblo at Tecochli. Two *gringo* men and a boy."

Having spoken his piece, the *pistolero* subsided into a lump still whiffing slightly of manure.

"Just so," said the Don. "It might be useful if you were to choose to visit *Senor* Thornhill as soon as possible. To inquire, perhaps, what might be the . . . intentions . . . of this Thornhill, and of those three of your countrymen."

Not much doubt about intentions. Intended to rob the damn mine, is what they intended, and Thornhill likely already paid well for his information.

"It is of interest, I believe," the Don added, "that the Bank of the Republic in Cuidad Juarez was robbed of thirty-seven thousand pesos seven weeks ago."

"Yes," Lee said, "I heard of that."

"And the thieves . . ."

"Yes . . ."

"Two men, and a boy as lookout."

Silence on the side porch of Mamacita's.

Nothing much more to say. Max Thornhill looked to be getting, say, thirty-five thousand pesos to set up a nice robbery of his employer's silver mine. Which meant that the mine office strong room must at present contain at least fifty to sixty thousand pesos' worth of refined silver bars.

More than enough to bring some very hard cases south from Texas. And longheaded thieves as well, to have robbed a bank very successfully and only to finance this present even more profitable venture.

"Why not send police up to the mine?"

The Don rolled his eyes slightly at such a *gringo* suggestion.

"My dear *Senor* McCann, the 'police' of this section of the Province are not 'police' in any ethical sense. They are, shall we say, servants of certain corrupt political groups, cabals, influences . . ."

So Lee hadn't been mistaken about Captain Gonsalves' speculative stare. "Certain corrupt political influences" surely included men like the Lieutenant Governor, a grim thug named Chavez, and just as certainly did not include friends of Don Luis. That wheel would turn, of course, but apparently not yet.

"Let us say then," said Don Jaime, "that it would be . . . unwise . . . to invite the police into the strong-room of the mine at Los Gatos."

And so, Don Jaime's visit to Mamacita's. Lee was, it appeared, to be the angel of salvation for Don Luis' silver at the Los Gatos mine. The angel of retribution as well, of course. In fact, the angel of death.

No use playing coy about it.

"I'll go to the mine directly and do what has to be done."

Don Jaime nodded, satisfied, and poured himself another cup of coffee. "I expected no less," he said, a considerable compliment from that source.

"One matter—these Americans . . ."

"I regret to say, very fierce. Savages. At Cuidad Juarez, they shot to death two men. It is our understanding that they killed a man at the pueblo of Tecochli also, and he himself had been a man of some reputation with firearms."

Worse and worse.

Not just a passel of border roughs with big eyes, then. The genuine article, they sounded. The McCoy. Hard cases driven south by the Rangers and the telegraph, by the county posses, the Federal Marshals and the Pinkertons. Driven south into wilder country. Country as wild as their country had been not too many years ago.

Three of them.

Wouldn't be like potting those sad, raggedy-ass *banditos* at Canyon Rojo. Wouldn't be like that at all . . .

Lee noticed that Don Jaime was scurrying to Las Sabrinas fast enough—taking his *pistolero* with him, too. Well, it wasn't fair to blame a man for being sensible.

Lee stood up from the table.

"My apologies," he said, "but it is a long ride to Los Gatos, and I had better be on my way." He held out his hand, and Don Jaime looked surprised, but took it.

"God go with you, *Senor*," Don Jaime said, "I will see that the young woman is. . . properly situated . . . at Las Sabrina."

God almighty—the old sissy thought Lee was for the bone-yard sure!

Chapter 10

Say what a man might of the black horse's looks, he was a locomotive for going; and just as well, for he had a piece to go before full dark, then a piece to go by moonlight before they were benighted.

And up and going again at dawn . . . then the last long climb up to Los Gatos. And make that before Thornhill left for his railroad train. Must get to Los Gatos before Thornhill left for his railroad train . . .

The girl had made no fuss at Lee's going, had understood she was to travel with Don Jaime and his people, had understood there would be work . . . a place to live.

Lee had kissed her. Her mouth was as soft as gardenia petals.

He swung up on the black—rifle and roll, war-bag and saddle-bag all tied to, canteen fresh filled with cold water—had waved to scrawny one-eyed Luz up on the porch, bent to lightly stroke the girl's soft black hair, then had spurred on out of the yard in a cackle of scooting chickens and had not looked back.

No call to. No use to.

The black had the damndest trot. If it weren't so steady a gait, a man would swear he was low-bucking.

Lee reined him down off the rock-strewn road and off into a stubbled cornfield, heading northeast by the sun. It was easier riding through the fields. Horse wasn't such a pounding ride.

This was pretty country, if you didn't mind it parched. Long as you didn't try to look long up into the hills for rich green, for big trees, pines and such . . . As long as you were content with scrub flowers, little juniper shrubs, that sort of stuff.

The evening was fine, though. Cooler than some. Night would be coming down before he was up into the hills at all. Lee was damned if he could accommodate to the black's gait. "You damned iron-leg son-of-a-bitch!" Lee tried booting the beast into a canter and the black did as he was bid, but wouldn't hold to it, slacked back into that grinding trot. Lee finally gave up on him. If the black wouldn't alter, then Lee's ass better had. He tried sitting looser, limper, rocking to the trot, and that did help some.

It appeared that with this horse, twenty-five years of riding, some twenty years of that work-riding, and some fifteen years of *that* breaking and training . . . Appeared that none of it was enough to deal with this damn horse.

Lee's back had commenced to ache like a boil.

At moonlight, higher in the country, Lee rode through a no-name village of little adobe whitewashed houses. Didn't look too bad, these little houses, unless you went inside. Then you wished you hadn't. Then you saw how poor the country was despite all the sunshine and the oranges easy to buy.

Nobody came out to see the wayfarer when the black's stone-hard hooves rang on the stones. These were not the villages, and night was not the time to be coming out of doors when a horseman came riding through. These *pueblos* had suffered in the Revolution—had seen their sons lined against church walls and shot. Had seen much worse things than that. No one from this nameless village cared to come outside to see who might be passing.

Lee rode through and rode on out by moonlight, riding higher all the time.

An moon-down, on a spiny ridge sharper than a toothed saw, Lee pulled the black up. The animal had kept to that grim gait of his for hours, and jarred Lee's guts near to entirely loose. But had not faltered, not mis-stepped. If it weren't for the pain of it, the black would be a considerable traveling horse.

Lee groaned aloud when he swung down out of the saddle. Felt his backside near skinned, his backbone a sore stick indeed. Cost him something to get the black hobbled, though the horse was well behaved enough. Just so damn sore.

He sat on a patch of a gamma (or at least the grass felt like gamma in the dark) and wolfed tortillas and handfuls of cold beans out of an oilskin package. Tasted damn good, too—almost took his mind off his aching butt.

Finished that, which didn't take long, he stumbled off into the dark to try and piss downhill, then stumbled back to his possibles, guided by the black's loud munching on the gamma or whatever. He tugged loose the Saltillo blanket, wrapped up in it as tight as any squaw, and lay down on the grass or whatever—felt mighty like rocks, in fact—and drifted off to a dire sleep and uneasy dreams.

He woke to the first of the light, saw through a drifting morning haze the narrow spine of the ridge stretching off north, up into the mountains, and sat up with a grunt —his rear still sore as spanked, the Saltillo jeweled with myriad drops of dew. The black stood, munching at pebbles apparently, a good distance off. It seemed to have broken its hobble in the night. Might stand still to be caught or might decide to lead Lee a little chase.

Looked to be a long day coming.

Whether it was the angle of the climb, or simply numbness in Lee's hindquarters, the black seemed easier riding today. They were up in real mountains now, for all there was no forest to ride through, and Lee's belly was grumbling for breakfast as he rode. There'd be no breakfast . . . no midday either. These mountains had odd streaks of ochre red running down through the rocks. Copper ore, perhaps. It was not a matter Lee cared to investigate. He'd had his run at copper years before.

Cooler up here, too.

This mountain, and then another—and then Los Gatos.

If the black didn't break a leg, which appeared unlikely from the way it had of stomping along like a donkey engine driving pilings. Lee leaned forward in the saddle, leaning into the climb as the black took a narrow pitch upslope. Would be a pleasure to get to the top of this one.

It was, of course, possible that Don Jaime and his information on Thornhill was so much horse shit. Thornhill might have family business . . . personal business . . . in Tampico. Might even have personal business in Buenos Aires.

Not likely, but possible.

Possible, also, that the wandering *Americano* hard-cases had had nothing in mind concerning Los Gatos. Might well have already wandered on. In which case, this damn ride was for nothing at all. In which case, Lee would be more than glad.

Hard to think another man could really put him down. Hard to think—but not impossible to think. Lee had known a couple of men who could certainly have put him down with knife or pistol. A couple of men . . .

You have the name, you can expect sooner or late to have to play the game. Had played it in Canyon Rojo, he supposed. And, he supposed, would have to play it at the mine in Los Gatos.

He reined the black right, higher up the slope. Perhaps an hour to the top of this shoulder . . . another two hours, or three to the reverse slope of the next mountain. Then another hour climbing to the top of that.

Maybe more than an hour.

He'd be lucky to ride in by the afternoon. Catch Thornhill there or at a switchback by Tenochli, if the fool had already caught the train. Catch Thornhill, and get the truth out of the son-of-a-bitch.

And then perhaps kill him? Perhaps. Don Luis would certainly be surprised if he didn't. Max Thornhill. No great loss—one of those foreigners who liked to lord it over the Mexs, made no nevermind he'd been born in the country himself. Spoke Spanish better, probably, than he did his father's German, his mother's English. Tall, ungainly fellow. Lee had met him once in Tenochli delivering a package of some kind —samples of silver ore, likely. Tall, awkward man with mild blue eyes . . . wore spectacles. Man had been pleasant enough to Lee at the time; hadn't pretended to be tough as so many men did who met Lee, made uneasy by him. Had been unpleasant to his Mexican assistant, though. Had made that fellow hop . . . made him look small before Lee.

It would be hard lines to take the fellow off the train. Could be done, but not easily. Much better to take him at the mine.

The black rumbled up and over the pitch at the mountain's shoulder, and Lee pulled him up for a breather, sat looking out at the second mountain. smaller, thank God. Less steep to it.

The black farted, bent its head, and started chewing on dwarf shrub of some kind. Greasewood, maybe. Creosote. Black didn't seem to give a damn. Chewed into it like bluegrass.

* * *

By afternoon—some twenty minutes after three o'clock by Lee's stem-winder— he rode the black up into Los Gatos. The black had been a fine grinder, one of the toughest Lee had ridden, but even this thick-boned nag was thoroughly worn out now, sweat- lathered and blowing. Lee's backside felt like a chunk of wood. He could reach back and pinch his butt and not feel that at all.

Los Gatos was a ruined village. It had been a small farming stead at one time, apparently. Now it was hutches and hovels for the mine workers, the *peons* who sweated in the refinery, the stamping mill. These men lived in Los Gatos as dogs lived in their kennels—going there to sleep, to eat some soggy trash or other, to get up at still dark and get to working.

Not a pueblo at all, really.

Some men, off-work, were standing in the narrow street today, gazing gap-mouthed as Lee urged the weary black along the cobbles. Took Lee a few moments to take these fellows in, to take in as well the silence of the place. No rythmic thud of the hammers up in the mill. No regular rumble as the ore was smashed to rubble.

Silence.

Sunday.

Of course—Thornhill would have planned the robbery for Sunday. Thornhill, or the others.

The men on the street stood or sat as still as near dead men, only their eyes, the slow turning of their heads showing otherwise as he rode by. They seemed barely curious.

No children. No women, either, though there were *cantinas* in the place—nasty, hot, tin-roofed sheds. A couple of them, the last time Lee had ridden through. There were women in those places, if you cared for toothless old women, other women so ripped and raddled with disease it took a very drunken man indeed to have anything to do with them. Some of these sad creatures had no noses, those members having rotted off or collapsed into the women's faces.

The liquor, the entertainments in these places, were of a primitive sort even by the standards Lee had known at the edges of the Rocky Mountains in deep winter. Fights between dogs and naked men . . . fights between drunks armed with broken bottles, the results wagered on.

He rode on up toward the mine . . . found himself wishing for another day, somehow, as if he were becoming shy . . . becoming more and more afraid of a fight. Of trouble. Better not be so. This was no time, no day for it.

He turned stiffly in the saddle, looking back at the men lined like statues along the streets. They would know, of course, of any three *Tejanos* in the place; no way those three could bury themselves deep enough not to be marked and remarked. These men would know, but they wouldn't be telling—certainly not telling another *gringo* (Don Luis' *gringo*) about those new *gringos*.

Pillars of silence, they would be, until it was over. Then they'd be pleased enough to mutter over it in their dens, get vomiting drunk on foul *mescal,* and stagger back to their sheds to dream of better villages, women, wives, children and other times.

Men who died in this place were not buried. They were escorted in shouting, stumbling processions, always at night between shifts, by small crowds of laughing drunks in torchlight. Carried out to the steep washes that drained the mountain-side in the winter rains, carried out on plank doors, prayed over by mock priests with the marks of the *penitentes* still laced across their backs.

They carried the fortunate-unfortunate out to one of these washes and dumped him down, cheering the fall. No scavengers but animal needed to crawl down to rob the corpses; that had long since been accomplished.

Tonight, very late, there would likely be another such parade. A celebration by moonlight . . .

Lee rode on out of the settlement, up the long, winding incline of the mine road, the black walking mighty slowly, out of steam at last.

Lee pulled the horse up and with some effort swung down from the saddle, lighting very stiff and stick-legged in the dirt. The black snorted, shook its head, and stood four-square and still, getting its breath.

"Well, you nail-gaited son-of-a-bitch, you got us here; damned if I know whether to thank you for it."

He led the black horse on up the mine road, trying as he walked to stretch his muscles loose, get some feeling back into his butt and legs . . . ease the reins-stiffness out of his fingers and hands.

Well, by God, if he didn't end by paying for this ride, someone else was surely going to do so. His painful ass was calling for vengeance of some sort, that was sure!

Chapter 11

He tied the black by a watering trough beside the settle-slide in the mine's lower yard. Slid the Winchester up and out of its scabbard, dug a box of ammunition from his saddle-bag and put it in his jacket pocket. Noticed then the buckskin was looking mighty worn. Not much the dandy, now. No wonder that grandee-steward had peered down his nose.

Standing there in the warm sunlight, he drew the Bisley, checking its loading, checked as well to see the cylinder spun free. Odd things seemed to happen to weapons sometimes on hard rides. Piece of road dirt, piece of turf kicked up, dust, mud. Stuff would seem to fly into the workings of a weapon to jam and slow its action.

Not this time. The Bisley Colt's maintained the action of a Switzerland watch.

Lee stooped a little to draw the broad-blade double-edge dagger from his right boot. Nothing to go wrong with that razor-sharp steel . . .

He slid the knife back into its sheath, then unstrapped his war-bag from the saddle cantle, reached in, and tugged free the coils of his whip. Draped those supple slender loops of braided black leather over his left shoulder. Never knew when a fine blacksnake lash might come in handy . . .

The mine building was a four-story tower, forty feet on a side. A considerable structure, this tower crowned the heights above Los Gatos as a castle might have done. It was pierced by windows here and there; at the top floor, the mine offices, and some places on down the rough plank walls, wherever the workings of hoists and chutes, steam engines and machinery required at least some good light.

A considerable building. Still and silent now. Sunday. No holiday since the revolution. Don Luis must have decided that one day's holiday at least was the better for production throughout the rest of the week.

A considerable building. And Thornhill's apartments on its fourth floor, behind the mine offices. Fellow had cared to be close to his work . . . .

Lee looked and finally saw a man standing in deep shadow up on the second level—

shadowed by the iron arm of a great crane. Man was watching him but not, it seemed, with much interest. Had a shotgun over his arm.

With such protection as this, no wonder Thornhill and his friends had planned a taking. Man up there looked barely awake.

Lee waved to the man to come down. Fellow stood still up there . . . moved not an inch as far as Lee could see. Lee picked up the Winchester. Waved again with that, and seemed to have an effect. Man with the shotgun turned to the long, angled flights of wooden steps to climb down to Lee's level and, to Lee's surprise, another guard, who must have been sleeping in the crane's shadow, stood up to follow his comrade.

Two guards, then. Two lazy fellows with shotguns to watch over a fortune in silver. Damned if he could blame Thornhill and the others. Too juicy a strike to pass up. Showed the weakness of the ways these people went about their business. Sooner pay a pack of spies to watch Thornhill than pay an extra two or three guards to make a robbery too risky.

Lee stood by the black, which had drunk some water from the trough, but not enough to founder itself (a knowing horse) and watched while these two guardian dragons shambled down the steps to him. A fair climb.

Then, at Lee's level, the two men padded

barefoot across the sun-baked yard to him —stupid, incurious as any of the work-broken men of the town. Round, flat Indian faces. Hooded, dull black eyes. Chosen, Lee supposed, for lack of any initiative, lack of the wit to comprehend the value of what they guarded, lack of the wit to plan to take it.

He didn't trouble to ask their names. Cared only that some fellow from Los Gatos didn't wander up to steal his goods off the black, steal the black itself.

"Do you know me?"

No answer. They stared at him like cattle.

"I am Don Luis' man." Lee put his hand on the coils of the whip at his shoulder.

What he said—or what he did—made some difference to them, and they nodded, attentive.

"You are to take this horse to the stable stalls behind the cracking shed. Do you understand me?"

Nods. Their eyes were on the coils of the whip.

"Do that, then resume your posts. If you sleep, I'll beat you. You understand that?"

Energetic nods—a muttered "*Si, Senor.*" Sad, ridden-down men, to take such threats, and them with shotguns in their hands.

Lee considered something, for the little good it might do.

"Have you seen other *Americanos* here?"

"No—no other *Americanos.*"

"If you see such," Lee said. "They are *banditos.* If you kill them, you may have their boots, their time-pieces. You understand?"

They nodded, looking uneasy. Not likely to be of much help. Still, as watch dogs, they might do to bark. Might be useful, just getting killed.

"*Senor* Thornhill—is he up in the building?"

"*Si.*" The "Patron" was in his building, the best news so far. No spurring the weary black downslope east to the switchback, then trying to climb that damn moving train.

"Go then," Lee said. "And do exactly as I have told you."

And off they trailed, looking more than a little worried, pausing to untie the black, to lead him away, apprehension in every line in their backs. Might have been a mistake to mention *Yanqui* banditos. New and sudden trouble was a thing no inhabitant of Los Gatos cared to hear about.

Hard to blame them.

Lee hefted the Winchester and walked over to the first long flight of wooden steps. A long climb to unpleasant work for the men of Los Gatos. Now, for him as well.

"I recall very well meeting you, Mister McCann. Though I can't conceive what might have brought you to Los Gatos. Surely not the nonsense you've been talking!"

A difficult interview.

Thornhill had been alone in the office, one large, square, sunny room lined with shelves of ore samples, heavy oak cabinets of files and other paper. Rows of high tables stacked with entry sheets, ore tags, weighing records, and pay receipts. The afternoon sunshine shone clear through this big room from side to side, turning slow, faint clouds of dust to gold.

Thornhill had, from the start, played so innocent and busy a fellow, so astonished at some nonsense about railroad tickets and steamship tickets, that Lee might almost have believed the Don's spies to have been sadly mistaken had not Thornhill mentioned Buenos Aires (in amused contempt at such a notion) before Lee had had a chance to do so.

So the foolish fellow had his plot indeed. The question now was the others.

The strong room was on the floor beneath this. Lee'd seen it. Heavier planking. Strips of iron spiked into the wall and door. Nothing, to be sure, to keep out a man with a charge of blasting powder. Not strong enough to keep out some determined men with axes, if it came to that, and they had time enough.

"Thornhill," Lee said, "I would surely

prefer not to kill you."

Thornhill, who had until then been rattling on like a barker at a county fair on the subject of trust and nonsensicality . . . the great difficulty of dealing with a primitive people of no real culture, no background in Europe whatsoever . . . suddenly shut his mouth.

Lee had never, so far as he knew, taken pleasure in seeing a man frightened. It was easy enough of a stunt, after all. Any fool with a revolver or a knife could accomplish it.

It gave him no joy, therefore, to see Thornhill (not a man of violence, after all) turn pale. No pleasure to see the man's hands tremble, resting on his desk top. Tall man, stooped now, his spectacle lenses reflecting the sunshine, the filing cabinets.

"I would prefer not to kill you but I certainly will do just that if you don't tell me where those hard-cases are right now."

Lee stood, waiting to see if the fellow was sensible.

Thornhill said nothing at all. Sat like a jackass in a cool mud pond. It was disturbing. It meant he was at least as scared of those fellows (whoever the hell they were) as he was of Lee.

"Now, now," Lee said, "don't be foolish. Don't force me to do what I'd rather not do . . ."

Thornhill reached up and took his spectacles off, held them in both his hands clutched close to his chest, as if Lee was bound to break them. The man then closed his eyes.

If Lee had not been so worried about those others, he might not have done what he then did, so soon.

He reached up to tug the whip free of his shoulder, drew his arm full back, and struck Thornhill across the face with the braided coils as hard as he could. Such an odd thing to do in a sunny business office.

Thornhill was knocked sideways out of the chair, still managing to hold his spectacles as he fell, and lay on his side on the floor, a stipple of bright blood appearing to bloom out of his face like tiny hibiscus blossoms. He drew a shuddering breath, opened his eyes, and stared up at Lee like an injured child as Lee stepped over above him to hit him again.

Lee struck down hard and Thornhill shouted something in some language—sounded like German to Lee—and with blood running from his nose as from a faucet, writhed and kicked in his fine grey suit, and rolled to hold onto Lee's right boot with both hands as if that would prevent him from being hit again—as if Lee might somehow protect him from Lee.

As much from shame as from exasperation with the man from being so uselessly stubborn, Lee kicked his boot free (striking

Thornhill in the side with the toe of it—not meaning to) and bent to beat the shouting fellow with the whip coils as a cowpoker might beat some trespasser with the coils of his lariat.

Scrambling away on his hands and knees under this punishment, trailing spatters of blood as he went, Thornhill again cried out in that foreign language and hustled full tilt into the side of a paper cabinet so that his head made a solid cracking sound against the oak.

Injured thus even more than Lee had injured him—likely thinking it was Lee had done it—Thornhill lay weeping, clutching his head where it had met the cabinet.

Lee bent over him, took him by his suit lapels heedless of the blood smeared on them and shook him out of his tears. Thornhill opened his eyes, lifted a shaking hand to wipe at them when Lee let him go, and then lay back on the floor, resigned, snot on his chin.

"Tell me," Lee said, "before I lose my patience."

Thornhill cleared his throat, then turned his head to the side and spat onto the floor. Lee saw that the man still had his spectacles clutched to his chest, still unbroken.

"They are camped east of Los Gatos," he said, sniffling as some drops of blood ran from his nose. He put up his hand to pinch at his nose to stop its bleeding. "And they will soon be here to kill you," he said with not a little satisfaction.

"Soon?"

"Soon enough," Thornhill said thickly. His nose was continuing to bleed a little.

"Who are they?"

Thornhill rolled an eye at him but didn't answer. The thought of Lee being murdered by those men had apparently given him courage.

Lee drew his knife, leaned down, and put the tip of the blade just under Thornhill's left eye. He pressed the blade tip in there, but only the smallest bit. "I surely will have your eye out of you like a mulberry if you don't give me any answers I ask for," Lee said. He had lost his patience.

"Pony Deal," Thornhill said. His eye was turning this way and that above the knife tip, as if it might manage somehow to escape its socket entirely.

"Deal?"

"Yes . . . a red-haired man."

Lee had heard of Deal, and nothing good. An Arizona gunman. Had been one of the Clanton people. And, Lee believed, had shot two men to death in McAllen, Texas. He'd heard of Deal.

"The others?" Expecting this time to be told that Wesley Hardin was out of prison and had come south to shoot Lee's buttons off. Hardin and Ben Thompson?

"Keller," Thornhill said. "A man named

Keller—and a boy. I don't know the boy's name." His eye looked wild.

At least it wasn't Hardin and Thompson.

Chapter 12

Lee sat at a window, looking out over the four-flight outside staircase—spidery wooden members laddering down, turning at a landing, then laddering down again, turn by turn, to the wide loading yard four stories down. The shadows were longer now —light would be going in an hour or two. Then dusk, then dark. It would be very unfortunate if those people came up to the mine by night. That would make matters very difficult.

It seemed unlikely, though. His own sad attempt at robbery had been at night and the result had been a dead deputy by lantern light.

The strong room, and its silver (Lee had gone downstairs to be certain the hen-house had not already been robbed) were on the floor below. Thornhill, bruised and swollen-nosed, all dignity fled, now sat on one stack of small silver bars, his hands tied behind him with office twine, his ankles tied together, and his ankles connected to his bound hands by another lashing. He was certainly uncomfortable but he was alive.

Don Luis would not approve.

It was barely possible for Lee to shoot a man to death and that man unarmed, and helpless.

It was certainly not impossible for him to beat a man until he broke.

Sadly for Don Luis' approval, however, Lee had found that he could not beat a man to flinders and then shoot him to death. So Thornhill, a stranger to the country he had been born in, now sat beaten on top of silver dug from its earth. Poor fellow was a ruined man and no mistake about it. A ruined man —and when his clerk and office staff, when other men who served the Don appeared with the new work week, would likely be a dead man. Someone would certainly seek to please the Don by taking Thornhill's head— and possibly in fact. Lee had heard of more than one *patron* who had demanded a very real head delivered to him in a basket.

A dead man perched on a stack of silver.

Unless his confederates came soon, unless they were able to kill Lee. Then, that done, if they were honorable men, they might free him. Might give him his share.

Might escort him safely to his train . . . see him off on his way to Tampico, the steamship, and Buenos Aires down in Argentina.

They might do that for Thornhill, but Lee wouldn't have cared to bet that way.

Lee had thought of staying down on the strong room floor, then had thought again. Here on the top floor he had the outside staircase under his gun—held the top of the inside staircase, too.

Good men with guns might well win their way into the strong room below. They'd play hell getting any silver out.

Don Luis would approve of that.

Time to wish Los Gatos was more than a company kennel. Time to wish it had a police post, friends of the Don or not. Even Captain Gonsalves would look good this afternoon. Gonsalves and his clever sergeant would both look mighty good.

Lee sat at his window, looking out, noticing the gleam of sunlight on the Winchester's barrel. Handsome weapon. Short ranged, though. Not like that old Sharp's.

An odd sound . . .

Odd sound.

It took Lee a moment to realize it was a human noise. It had sounded like machinery . . . whining . . . unoiled. Not that, though. Not machinery.

A man screaming down in the yard.

A high, thin, screeching noise. A trapped rabbit's scream.

Lee levered the Winchester and stepped back out of the window light.

Silence. No more screaming from the yard.

They must have caught one of those sad, stupid guards. Played at him with a knife, it sounded. Lee didn't doubt the poor fellow had said all he knew before they cut his throat for him—let him shriek out that last scream for Lee to hear.

Some relief they hadn't waited till night. Some relief, but not much. For the guard, no relief at all.

Someone shouted in the yard, voice echoing from the buildings' sides. Something in Spanish. Shouted again.

Lee was ashamed that he jumped a little when a shotgun went off down in the yard. No doubt about that hard slamming sound.

A revolver shot came right after.

Both guards down. Lee was surprised the second man had made any showing at all. There'd been a man behind that dull stare, after all, a man who could hear his fellow die screaming like a rabbit and still come on.

Lee stepped back to the window and saw, down in the yard, a man in cowhide chaps standing looking up at him. Man had a Stetson hanging down his back on its chincord. Had a shock of red hair. Sunburned face, with a lank, jutting jaw. Too far to see the color of his eyes. Wore two revolvers—

looked like Remingtons from the butts—
holstered high at his sides.

Deal, Lee supposed.

Man waved up at him. Seemed to be
smiling.

"Sent for the cavalry, did they?"

Odd, that the first thing Lee should feel
just for an instant was pleasure at hearing
an American voice. It lifted his spirits, no
question of it.

He stood to the side of the window, carefully, and called back down.

"Sent for—and come! You Deal?"

Though he was watching, Lee didn't see
Deal draw. Saw the powder-smoke at the
American's left hand, and flinched away as
the side of the window frame splintered,
smashed.

Lee leaned out fast with the Winchester
to squeeze off his shot just as Deal skipped
back under the shadow of the stairway.
Saw the round kick dust just behind the
man's heel.

Silence then for a while.

Lee levered another round into the Winchester. If Deal had made a slightly better
shot than that, Lee would be cold meat. Son
of a bitch was every bit as good as Lee had
worried. No sign of the other men, though.
Man and boy.

"Say!" Deal called from below, "Sorry
about that cheap shot, McCann. It is

'McCann,' ain't it?"

"It is!" Lee called back, and heard Deal say something to someone else in the yard.

"I suppose," Deal called up again. "—I suppose you've seen that old elephant, McCann!"

"I have, and walked 'round it and kicked its ass."

"So I thought . . ."

Lee leaned to the window again, saw that Deal was staying snug out of sight while he did his shouting.

"And that being so," Deal called, "you must surely be an open-minded fellow. Open to . . . say . . . thirty thousand pesos? Just to arrive here the littlest bit too late?"

"And what about Thornhill?"

Deal laughed. Lee again heard him say something to someone in the yard.

"You don't say that dude is still kickin'?"

"Still waiting for his *compadres*," Lee called.

Deal laughed again. "Sorry to cross a pal," he shouted, "but I'll just pass them pesos over to you, McCann—do you earn them!"

Lee was a little surprised that Deal and his men hadn't made a harder try. Was not surprised that they knew his name, at least the name he was using. Thornhill must have stooled his guts, mentioned Lee as a possible tripping block. For whatever reason, perhaps some notion that Lee might be stupid enough to trust him, Deal had tried his first shot—and a fair enough shot it had been—and then gone to talking.

Deal apparently took silence for encouragement.

"Say—McCann?"

"I'm here."

"I suppose you wouldn't care to have me come up an' talk to you. I could bring that passel of pesos with me . . ."

"Come right on up."

Deal laughed. A merry man, apparently. "I do, an' you'll plug me. Right?"

"That's right," Lee said.

"Didn't hear yuh!"

"I said, *you're right!*"

Deal thought that over for a moment or two. Then Lee heard him call, "Matty!" to someone down there.

Lee leaned to the window, seeing if there might be a shot to take while Deal was so busy chatting. Saw nothing at first. Long shadows stretching across the yard. Then a moving shadow at the base of the outside stairs. One of them coming out.

Lee leveled the Winchester down.

Saw a white piece of cloth. A tow-headed kid waving a white piece of cloth. This boy came stepping right out under Lee's gun waving that foolish piece of rag in both hands. Came out and walked to the bottom of the staircase and started climbing right up as if he was going to a barn dance.

There'd been an instant there when Lee should have shot him, and damn that white cloth. But the boy had no gun showing. Had looked mighty young to be in such desperate company. It crossed Lee's mind that Deal and Keller might be forcing the kid along.

Mister Keller seemed to be a little shy.

The boy had reached the second landing now—looked up at Lee and waved the silly scrap of cloth again. Appeared some sort of Reuben farm boy, fifteen years old, if that. Yellow hair and a face full of freckles. Homely as a hedge fence.

Boy was carrying a small canvas bank sack. Lee could see some printing across the canvas. That, he supposed, would be the pesos Deal intended to buy him with. It was no temptation, particularly since Deal would certainly back-shoot him at the first opportunity thereafter and take those pesos right back.

Time now to shoot the boy, if he was going to.

Kid was coming up the last flight of steps, leaving a long late-afternoon shadow behind him.

"Take it easy now, McCann . . . !" Deal worried about that timely shot. "Matty's just got your cash money there. No need to be pluggin' a kid."

Lee said nothing.

"No need to go jumpy, now . . ." Deal

sounded some jumpy, himself. Liked the boy, apparently.

"Mister . . .?"

The farm boy stood just below Lee's window on the last landing, ten feet away, and dead meat.

"I got your money, Mister. Pony wants you to come down and get off this place. We won't bother you none do you do it . . ."

The boy was dressed mighty poorly for having been in a big bank robbery. Likely the three of them hadn't had the chance to buy much in the way of pretties, hustling down here for the bigger score. Boy was in worn blue-jean trousers and baggy flannel shirt, skinny wrists and ankles sticking out like a scarecrow's.

Not a rich target at ten feet.

"Kid," Lee said, keeping to the side of the window in case Deal tried his luck again, "kid, you'd better get your butt back down those steps . . ."

"I got your money," the kid said, dumb as a dog, and started up the last flight of steps to the door, still waving the white rag at Lee as if it was magic.

Lee stepped over to the door, turned the knob, and pulled it wide open. Might do to knock the kid silly . . . tie him up . . .

The boy stood squinting in the sunlight. He held the bank-bag out to Lee as if he'd been sent for, was handing over a bucket of beer.

"You come in here," Lee said. "You won't be going back down those steps."

The boy heard him out, then shook his head as stubbornly and stupidly as a horse, held the bank-bag out for Lee to take. The boy had light grey eyes.

Lee started to take the long step out onto the landing to get his hand on the kid and haul him in—and stopped. There was a noise . . . something . . . behind him.

Lee half turned, heard a ticking . . . something back in the office. A sound down the inside staircase.

Keller. And the reason for all the talk.

He glanced at the boy to judge him for a stroke of the Winchester's butt and saw him standing as he had been, but now the bank-bag falling to the planking. The boy was still clutching the white cloth with his left hand and reaching behind his back with his right.

Lee leveled the rifle and shot the kid through the belly.

He had almost turned back into the office when a slight young man with long black hair to his shoulders, dressed like a drover—a blue bandana 'round his neck—came up the inside stairs and into the office firing revolvers right and left.

This man's first shot caught Lee along his left side and spun him into the door frame. The second struck the Winchester's receiver and blew the rifle from Lee's hand.

Felt as though his wrist was broken.

Lee threw himself down behind a row of sample tables, trying to reach around to get his left hand on the Bisley Colt's. The long-haired young man came across the office at him at a run—boots sounded like thunder on the floor.

Lee got the Bisley out of its holster cross-handed, knelt up and shot the young man high through the chest. But Keller—ex-drover, bank robber, whatever—was the McCoy. He went back-stepping 'til a desk stopped him, and fired left and right as he did. The sombrero was snatched from Lee's head as if by a hasty wind, and he stood and fired back, shooting left-handed into a cloud of gunsmoke. The round struck Keller at the side of his forehead and seemed to blow a piece of his skull away.

The long-haired man fell sideways in a quick bright spray of blood and, lying on the floor, raised his right-hand gun and fired at Lee again, as if his injury, looking so desperate, was nothing much after all.

Lee shouted . . . something. He stooped as Keller fired again, the bullet snapping past Lee's left ear, stooped lower still to get a clear shot under the powder smoke, and caught that surprising fellow up on his knees, clutching the side of an office desk, trying to get to his feet.

Lee, frightened as he had ever been in a fight, then shot Keller once through the middle to hold him still, then a second time, this round striking Keller in the head with a sharp whacking sound and killing him.

Lee stood upright, staggered and almost fell. His left side hurt like blazes. Felt like that young son-of-a-bitch had shot a rib out of him. Damned if Lee had ever seen a fellow more determined in a fight. Damned if he had!

The office was full of smoke. They'd done some shooting, no saying they hadn't. That Keller—and who had ever heard of him— pure poison in a fight.

Someone screaming like a woman.

Not Keller, please God. That son-of-a-bitch was finally dead as any man ever had been.

Someone screaming, though.

Lee walked to the door. He could see through the smoke to the landing outside. Tried to reload the Bisley one-handed as he went—an awkward business. Felt as if his right wrist was broken from that second shot. The Winchester surely a dead loss. Don Luis could fucking well pay for a replacement.

Screaming . . .

Lee stood in the doorway, off to a side so that Deal mightn't get a shot from below, and saw the boy standing down on the second landing. He had apparently torn his shirt open to get at the place where Lee had shot him and now stood wailing, both hands fumbling at his bright red belly where a thick, soft tube of red and blue came bulging out, spattering blood down his blue-jean trousers. At his narrow chest, revealed by the opened shirt, two small long-nippled breasts trembled at each scream.

A girl, of course. *"Mattie."* And Lee should have known it. Thin, fragile wrists on a farm boy . . .

The girl, her hands clenched in the complications of her guts where the rifle bullet had undone her, put her head back, staring up as if some mercy might be expected from the sky, and called out, as regular as a clock, the same high trilling shriek.

There were clots of brown down the steps, the way she'd gone, her torn bowels releasing what they'd held.

A little nickel-plated revolver lay on the second step. Kept it behind her back, tucked into her pants as she held the bankbag out. The bag lay on the landing at Lee's feet.

"Oh, Mattie . . . *Oh, Mattie!"*

Deal was getting his reward, shouting up at the screaming girl. There was that in his voice was worse than the agony in hers. And the only way up to her was into Lee's gun.

Smoke came swirling out of the office behind Lee, thicker than it had been in the fight and smelling of wood and paint and coal oil, not gunpowder.

Keller had set a fire down below—or Deal had, once Keller was climbing. Had figured to smoke Lee out, if shooting didn't do the trick.

The mine building was burning up its four stories like a chimney. Deal and Keller must have thought there'd be just time enough to get the silver out once Lee was flushed.

But Lee wasn't flushed.

The girl stopped making her noise and sank to her knees. Her hands were full of herself now. Blood everywhere down there.

Lee cocked the Bisley to finish her, but Deal got in first from below. One shot up and through her heart, it seemed. Knocked her over and gone, and not a kick.

"*Oh . . . Mattie . . .*"

Should never have sent her up—should never have brought her to Los Gatos. Lee felt sorry for the man. Hard not to.

"Sorry, Deal," he called down. "*Bad business all 'round.*"

Deal came out and up the steps like a cougar, a revolver in each hand, but only the left one firing. Must be a lefty.

Lee fired a fast shot and missed Deal plenty. Then Deal was at the second landing, fired that left-hand Remington twice, clipped Lee through the calf of his right leg, and knocked him down.

Lee landed as if he'd been dropped some

distance, landed hard enough to knock his wind out—the shot leg didn't pain at all— and fired from there and missed again as Deal jumped past the girl's body, leveling that Remington for a finisher. Jumped almost past the girl's body. Deal's boot slipped in the blood.

Deal went to one knee—had to drop his right-hand gun to steady himself, to lever himself up again, quick as a cat. He didn't drop the left-hand gun.

Lee, still stretched out and out of breath, sighted along the length of his hurt leg and shot Deal through the throat as the red-haired man came lunging up the steps again, cowhide chaps flapping, the left-hand Remington coming down to the level.

The bullet struck Deal just under his long, pale sunburned jaw to the right of his Adam's apple, and knocked a small black hole clear through his neck, front to back.

The small hole turned immediately red as an angry eye, and spurted a thin squirt of blood before Deal as he kept coming and fired at Lee as Lee rolled left for his life.

A plank split and brushed out splinters with a crash as Lee's head jerked just enough away, and Lee raised the Bisley and shot Deal again, straight into the man's chest as he came on.

Deal stumbled and drew a great whooping breath. Then he seemed to recover and came up the last two steps, but slower. Got to the landing and tripped again. Said, "No . . . *no*," and staggered toward the staircase railing as if Lee wasn't lying there at all, close enough to reach out and touch.

Deal drew that noisy breath again, opened his left hand and let the revolver fall out of it. The heavy weapon made a heavy sound striking the planks.

Deal, his back to Lee, clung to the staircase railing with both hands, and drew another long, noisy breath. His dirty checkered shirt was half soaked with blood from the wound through his neck.

Lee, propped up on an elbow, lifted the Bisley Colt's, cocked it, and fired into Deal's back and broke it.

Chapter 13

It took a while for Lee to get up.

The leg had had no feeling to it for a time —couldn't make the thing work. Lee would have preferred pain to not being able to stand at all.

But that didn't last. Soon enough, he could make the leg answer him. The pain came with that, though, and then Lee would have preferred crawling.

The smoke was rolling out onto the staircase landing. A soft, continuous thumping sound like a dull roll of drums sounded from inside the building. The Los Gatos mine was burning. Lee, supporting himself on the stairway railing as Deal had, looked down the building's side and saw flickering red at the lower windows. He put his arm out, rested his head against the building's

side. Warm—warmer than the dying sunlight would have made it. Eddies of smoke
drifted past him, over him—over the two
dead ones, too. Deal at his feet was
stretched out as if he was asleep, having
bathed in red. Man was not as tall lying
there as he had been coming up the steps,
shooting. Might have done better standing
still to shoot rather than firing as he had, on
the climb. Had he done any better though,
Lee would be stony dead instead of just
crippled up and hurting.

The girl lay huddled down on the second
story landing, dead in a tangle of her guts.

Lee looked down there once and didn't
look again.

Not my fault. Not my fault . . .

Smoke, rich and dark grey as unmilked
chocolate, was rolling out of the fourth floor
doorway now like a thunderhead, with a
soft, roaring sound, as if the smoke was
being breathed out by a beast somewhere
inside. There was nothing welcoming about
it.

Inside, one full floor down and barred
behind strong oak doors banded with iron
straps, Thornhill would be sitting on his
stack of silver bars, hearing the fire coming
up around him, smelling the smoke, seeing
the first hazy tendrils of it drifting under
the weighty doors. Would be hot down
there, now, growing swiftly hotter as if

some great furnace door was slowly swinging wide.

In a short while, the strong room would be broken by the fire, the iron bands turning dull cherry, the thick oak panels charring, glowing their own cheery crimson in the flames.

The doors, the walls would then buckle like a drunken woman to a man's embraces, and the fire would come in upon Thornhill and torment the bound man to squalling. Torment him into something much less than human before his brain baked hard as a hard-cooked egg, the stack of silver molten beneath his roasted corpse. Spectacle frames running in bright drops of liquid gold.

Lee had tied him. Lee had left him there.

Lee turned from the rail, the splintering wood already hot beneath his hand, and limping wonderfully (dipping and swaying at each step as if he were at sea in very heavy weather) he managed to get to the doorway—drew in as deep a breath of air as he could—and dragged his furious leg along into smoke and the mine office.

It was a long walk to the inside stairs. A blind walk. Lee had heard of the darkness of fires; this was his first experience of it.

The world was dark, velvety grey, a single sheet of that color wherever he chose to look. Lee put his hand up to his face and could not see it. Couldn't see it when his fingertips were brushing his eyelids.

He felt his way across the room, his boot soles growing hot enough to burn him, his shot-through leg giving him fits. His side, where Keller had clipped him, hardly bothered him at all in comparison. Lee felt his way across the office (and a damned wide office it seemed) by crashing into desks and tables, by nearly tripping over this chair and that file-box—did trip over Keller all of a sudden, and almost fell. His hurt leg, his aching lungs were both telling him not to fall. Not to fall down and lose his sense of where the staircase was . . . not to fall and forget where the door lay behind him . . .

Not to forget that.

Keller had felt companionably soft to the toe of his boot when it struck him. Even a dead man was good company in this grey world of no breathing, though Lee's chest had begun an odd sort of trying to breathe whether he wished it to or not.

Lee reached the inside staircase—and knew it because a savage wind of heat was pouring up from the stairwell, all unseen in the cool, cool grey.

The heat burned his face as scalding water would have done; Lee smelled his hair as it began to burn . . . the softer stink of scorching buckskin as his jacket began to char.

"Walk in to me, and die," that strong wind said.

Lee stood for a moment, blind at the top of the stairs—tried to turn his face from the heat, and felt the skin begin to blister on his cheek, his ear.

"Walk on down . . . and die."

The building trembled beneath him, the fire shaking it as a cat might shake a chipmunk it had caught among spring grasses.

Lee leaned into the wind as best he was able, fumbled for a hold on the stair railing, and jerked his hand away from rounded wood hot as any stove lid.

"Thornhill!" He shouted the man's name again. Screamed the man's name down the thundering well of fire, bright enough now to lighten even the perfect grey to a brighter shade.

"THORNHILL!"

And turned away, not knowing whether it was the fire or the wound in his leg that pained him so. Felt as if a pack of dogs were tearing at him.

But turned away.

Not such a champion, after all . . .

Man could never have heard him, of course. Was, more than likely, already dead. Been foolish, no doubt, even to come in to try for him.

A foolish gunman. Happy enough to be shooting girls; not so pleased, however, to go down into fire to save a man he had left bound and helpless. Not so pleased to be doing that . . .

Lee was sure he had properly turned around, had properly retraced his path. It was puzzling how long it took a man with a dreadful leg to drag it through brightening grey toward a door that better be there.

It took the longest time a man could think of.

Lee tried to take in just a little breath— the smallest sip of a breath. Just once.

The grey slipped into his lungs and tore at them like a gardening rake. Lee whined in his throat, then. Whined like a dog begging to be let in from winter.

Perhaps it was the pain of his leg that helped him a little, kept his mind on what he was doing. On where he was, and what was happening. His leg kept him from dreaming in the grey while he spent a long, long lifetime crossing thirty feet of planking. The planking hissed and spat, popped and cracked beneath his boots as he limped along, stumbling from this smoking table to that charring chair.

Never bumped into Keller going back. Thought at the time that the dead bandit had gotten up somehow and walked out of the fire and on out a window perhaps. On out into the cool air.

Lee found the door as he was dying, tripped over the sill, staggered onto the landing, and fell full length into a vagrant draft of clear wind blowing hard into the welcoming flames.

Senor Saumarez had been a *regulator*, a conductor and inspector of the wheels and carriages on the railways of the Republic for some twenty-three years. Had, of course, seen extraordinary sights in that long time, sights that the average peasant, stuck like a mole in his little piece of dirt, could hardly imagine. It was quite correct, what some Englishman had said about travel. It did broaden a man, enrich him, make him more of a man.

There were rich men who hadn't seen of the Republic what Miguel Saumarez had seen. Nor was landscape, town-scape, city-scape all of travel's pleasures. Not nearly.

Men—women—children. Here were land-scapes that a wise man could never fail to profit from.

Were there many who had seen Juarez writing in his notebooks in the public car on the Sinaloa grade?

Not many.

Not many who had been shot twice by varieties of bandit-politicos, both wounds being received in attacks upon the railroad by men too ignorant to perceive its most essential value to a civilized state. Shot twice, and awarded medals for each wound.

Men, women, and children. Not many men (and they could thank God and His

Mother for it) had seen a child crushed under the great flanged wheels for playing unwisely in the grand Station at Mexico City. Not many—and they could thank God again—who had seen that child's mother go mad at the sight.

An official, a man of honor and responsibility, speaks to no-one of more private visions—of innumerable matters of sexual intercourse in this carriage or that, and by no means always in the third class.

And a murder, still unsolved. A Brazilian, speaking a very comic Spanish, a generous tipper and a gentleman, found lying quite dead, a knife driven into his back so thoroughly that the policeman, later, had had to plant his shoe between the poor fellow's shoulderblades and heave him like a black to free it.

A bad business. The Brazilian had offended no-one, as far as a man could recall . . .

Strange events and much traveling—but few stranger than this of tonight, when an undoubted *Tejano*, stinking of smoke, his trouser leg a column of blood (more blood still at the left side of his jacket) had hauled himself aboard by moonlight at the switchback ten miles from Los Gatos. Had left a fine if somewhat stocky black horse trotting free behind him also, and not seemed to care.

A dentist named Fernandez had been

smoking on the platform, and had, to his surprise, received from the night air—saddlebags (from one of which, he confided, a corner of a more official canvas sack appeared, which jingled in a way that only pesos do.) He then received right after a call for assistance, which he gave, helping to pull this bedraggled *gringo* (obviously having been up to much less than good) off his sturdy black horse and onto the rear platform of the *Especial.* And fortunate he had not attempted this at a straight-away where the train might have been speeding to fifty kilometers an hour.

This much the dentist had seen and done, and Saumarez had not.

The rest of the matter, however, was railroad business and no business of the dentist who, it seemed, lacked a little in the understanding of proper procedure and private communication.

Once this importunate dentist, however, was shut out of a compartment in the first class, the *Yanqui* was able to establish to a *regulator's* satisfaction a fine sense of the fitness of things, requesting permission to stay on board (apologizing handsomely for his unorthodox method of mounting) and offering immediately to pay both for that very first class compartment and for the undoubted inconvenience to the *regulator* of this surprising style of commencing a railroad journey.

The fellow had looked sadly used enough, after all, and Miguel Saumarez, while he knew his duty, was also a Christian.

The gringo appeared drunk at first, though it soon became apparent that he was only sad, and sadly scorched and wounded. Had something to say about a dog, and the removal of a dog's collar, then asked if a *medico* might be traveling. Asked also the names of shipping companies that might own vessels out of Tampico for the Argentine trade.

An odd fellow, even for a *Yanqui*. A bandit of some sort, Saumarez had supposed, though in these troubled times, who was there who was *not* a bandit of some sort?

The *medico*, a physician named Lopez traveling with his wife from Hermosillo, was very rude when asked later for information perfectly proper for a railroad official to possess.

It could only be said with certainty—since just before morning, passing the compartment, it had accidently been overheard—that this *gringo* had wept.

From the pain of his injuries, no doubt.

A man of violence, a foreigner, and a Protestant must surely expect some punishment for the error of his ways.

MAKE SURE YOU HAVE ALL THE BOOKS IN LEISURE'S RED-HOT *BUCKSKIN* SERIES

Make the Most of Your Leisure Time with
LEISURE BOOKS

Please send me the following titles:

Quantity	Book Number	Price
_____	_____	_____
_____	_____	_____
_____	_____	_____
_____	_____	_____

If out of stock on any of the above titles, please send me the alternate title(s) listed below:

_____	_____	_____
_____	_____	_____
_____	_____	_____

Postage & Handling _____

Total Enclosed $ _____

☐ Please send me a free catalog.

NAME _____
(please print)

ADDRESS _____

CITY _____ STATE _____ ZIP _____

Please include $1.00 shipping and handling for the first book ordered and 25¢ for each book thereafter in the same order. All orders are shipped within approximately 4 weeks via postal service book rate. PAYMENT MUST ACCOMPANY ALL ORDERS.*

*Canadian orders must be paid in US dollars payable through a New York banking facility.

Mail coupon to: **Dorchester Publishing Co., Inc.**
6 East 39 Street, Suite 900
New York, NY 10016
Att: ORDER DEPT.